Unwanted Guest

Albert Moose

Contents

Prologue

Raizada Mansion, New Delhi

3.40 am

.

The main door of the huge mansion was opened and a girl in her early twenties tiptoed to the living hall. The entire house was in darkness and she lit her torch light.

Sighing in relief she walked forward but froze on her steps when the lights were turned on.

Closing her eyes tightly she turned and bend her head down. "Sorry uncle" she whispered.

"What's the time now?" a very angry Akash Singh Raizada asked crossing his arms.

She looked at her mobile and said, "3.40"

"Is this the time you walk into a house Aisha?" Akash shouted.

"Woh...my car broke down and I got a mechanic to fix it...then..." Aisha mumbled.

"And this shirt you're wearing must be of that mechanic, I assume" Akash scoffed looking at the oversized shirt she was wearing.

Aisha gulped and Akash said, "I'll have to talk to your parents"

"Woh main..." Aisha cried.

Akash showed his palm and said, "We allowed you in this house just because of your mother Lavanya. Lavanya is dear to us all and she wanted us to look after you till you complete your studies! It's just three months that you're here and you've already started to stay out during nights....with mechanics!"

"He is my boyfriend" Aisha said in tears.

"Go to your room!" Akash said sternly.

"Please..."

"Aisha go" Akash said pointing to the stairs.

.

.

.

8.45 am

.

"I don't like that girl!" Anjali said disgusted, "I'm just tolerating her for Lavanya!"

"How on earth did Lavanya have such a spoilt daughter?" Mami asked shaking her head.

"Aur nahi to kya" Anjali said, "Out at late night and that too with a boy!"

"She said it's her boyfriend" Akash said biting his toast.

"Chiiii....girls these days...have no culture at all!" Mami cried.

"Dadi, even I go for parties!" Ayush, Akash and Payal's son said.

"You're a boy Ayush" Anjali said, "She is a girl!"

"Why are you all getting hyper on that?" Payal said sighing, "It's her life. Let her live it on her terms"

"What?" Akash cried, "Lavanya has trusted her daughter with us Payal. It's our responsibility to keep her safe!"

Payal said, "When she said keep her safe, she meant giving her shelter and providing her care. She didn't ask you to be her father and ban her from going to parties with her boyfriend!"

"But..." Anjali began to say something but stopped seeing Aisha walking to the living room.

"Good morning everyone" she said slowly.

"Good morning Aisha, sit" Payal said smiling. Aisha smiled and sat next to Ayush. "Good morning" Ayush said smiling. "Good morning Ayush" Aisha smiled.

"Aisha, HP was telling me that your car isn't there outside" Payal said.

"Ha ma, woh it broke down. I have taken it to garage!" Aisha said.

"Ma? Again?" Akash said shaking his head, "I've asked you to stop calling her that didn't I?"

"Akash" Payal hissed, "It's fine Aisha. You can call me that!" she said caressing her hair. Aisha smiled faintly and looked at Akash, Anjali and Mami who were glaring at her.

Ayush cleared his throat and asked, "So Aisha how are you going to reach college?"

"I'll catch an auto" Aisha said.

"I can drop you. It's on the way" Ayush said.

"Nahi it's fine I'll...." Aisha began when Payal said, "Go na...he'll drop you!"

Aisha sighed and nodded.

"Let's go" Ayush said standing up and Aisha nodded. She stood up and Payal said, "But you didn't eat anything"

She grabbed a sandwich and said, "I'll eat on my way. Bye ma!" she hugged Payal.

"Bye ma...bye everyone" Ayush said and walked out with Aisha.

"Akash, keep your son away from that girl" Anjali said crunching her face.

"Ha Ayush seems to be very lovely dovey with her" Mami said.

"They are just friends" Payal said sighing. This family will surely drive her to nuts. She walked to the kitchen to help HP.

She looked back to find Anjali and mami feeding bad about Aisha to Akash. She shook her head and said aloud, "What did that girl even do to you guys that you hate her so much? Just because she comes home late and spends time with her boyfriend, she is a slut! And when Ayush does the same, you don't find anything wrong! It shows how low you are, not her!" and she stormed inside angrily.

Chapter 1

AR Headquarters, New Delhi

11.30 am

.

"How are the new interns?" Akash asked not taking his eyes from the files.

"Average" Aman Mathur, his PA, said, "But a few are very good. It's not very hard to pick students who have natural interest in fashion designing from a batch of idiots!" he forwarded few papers to Akash and said, "The designer head gave me this. These are the ones she selected from the group!"

Akash went through the designs and said, "These are designed by the interns?" Akash asked surprised.

"Yeah, two of them. Others are just failures!" Aman said shaking his head.

Akash nodded and said, "So Aman, my plan is...since we had promised the National Fashion Institution, Delhi, that we would give their students certified internship, we should definitely give them that, no matter if the students are poor or not. But I would like the best of those students to work for AR as an extended internship!"

Aman nodded and asked, "So this one week internship?"

"Every student can attend that" Akash said, "But the selected ones can work for AR for our upcoming show, after this one week internship. Go and inform them about the same!"

"So we're selecting those two who made these designs?" Aman asked pointing to the papers.

Akash nodded and said surprised, "I've never seen such beautiful designs for so long. Exceptionally well, especially this lehenga....beautiful. Who designed this? I've only seen such designs from..." he stopped himself.

"From ASR" Aman whispered completing him.

Akash took a deep breath and nodded, "ASR" he whispered.

"I'll inform the students" Aman said and Akash looked up at him. "What are their names?"

Aman looked down to his file and said, "Ayan Sharma and Aisha Shrivastav"

"Aisha Shrivastav" Akash asked shocked.

Aman looked up from the file and asked surprised of his face, "Yeah, you know her?"

"Yeah, she is Lavanya's daughter, staying at my home. Remember I told you?"

"Ah, the girl who stays out late at night and the one whom your family hates for the very same reason?" Aman asked chuckling.

Akash sighed and said, "Yeah"

Aman shook his head and was about to walk out when Akash asked, "Any news about them?"

Aman looked at him and nodded no. Akash sighed and Aman said, "It's been 23 years Akash. I think they don't want to be found. If otherwise our detectives would have tracked them down. ASR was the best businessman of his times. It would've been an easy task to hunt him down...if only he was willing to be found."

Akash nodded and Aman walked out.

.

.

.

Raizada Mansion, New Delhi

8.30 pm

.

"You should take rest dear. HP is here to help me" Payal said smiling. "Nahi it's fine. I like helping" Aisha said smiling and continued peeling potatoes.

"How was your day at college?"

"They took us to AR" she said. "AR?" Payal asked surprised.

Aisha smiled and said, "AR is offering us one week internship. So our college took us there and internship starts tomorrow!"

"That's great" Payal said.

"There's more" Aisha said smiling widely, "We were all asked to design a lehenga. And they selected two from our batch to work for the upcoming show!"

"And lemme guess, you're in the two!" Payal said chuckling.

"Ha" Aisha squealed and Payal hugged her, "Congratulations"

"Thank you Ma!" Aisha said happily.

"It's a great opportunity. A certificate of AR Fashions will guarantee you a job at any fashion house!" Payal said smiling.

"Even mamma said the same" Aisha said smiling.

"Waise you returned early today. Didn't go out with Ayan?" Payal asked.

Aisha smiled sheepishly and said, "Yesterday it was a birthday party. That's why I was late."

"When did I ask that?" Payal asked laughing. Aisha bit her lip and giggled. "He has to visit a friend of his"

"Waise...." Aisha asked, "Why does Anjali aunty ask Ayush to call her ma?"

Payal froze and looked at her. "When did you hear that?" she asked.

Aisha stopped peeling the potatoes and looked at her. "Woh, I was passing by his room and heard her...what happened ma? Is everything okay?"

"Yeah...it's...nothing" Payal shook her head and continued stirring the curry.

Aisha hummed and continued peeling potatoes but her eyes fixed on Payal. "Woh" she said, "I thought...since I call you ma...she thought why not Ayush call her...."

"Stop talking Aisha" Payal mumbled, "I'm not in a good mood and I definitely don't want to hear about that woman"

Aisha was taken aback and she looked down to the potatoes.

"Ma" Ayush said cheerfully walking into the kitchen, "Oh hello Aisha!"

"Hello" Aisha said smiling.

"How was college?" he asked sitting on the kitchen slab and peeping to what Payal was cooking.

"She got selected to work for AR as intern and get down Ayush!" Payal said smacking her son's arm.

"Ouch..." Ayush said and jumped down, "Congrats Aisha!"

"Thanks" she said.

"Learn something from her" Payal said smacking his head, "Look at you. The backbencher!"

"Fashion designing is easier than BTech Ma!" Ayush whined. Aisha giggled and Ayush whispered to her, "Save me please. Or else ma will begin her lecture on how every course in this universe is similar and same!"

Aisha hid her laughter and said, "Ha ma, fashion designing is much easier!"

"See" Ayush cried.

Payal rolled her eyes and Aisha said, "Chalo, I've completed the potatoes. Ma, let me go and make a call to home!"

"Ha dear" Payal said and Aisha walked out.

Ayush waited for her to leave and said after she left, "Anjali bua is very irritating"

"Aisha told me" Payal said, "She asked you to call her ma?"

"Ha" Ayush said irritated, "She began her usual pep talk on how she is a good mother and looked after me when I was a baby. How she is better than you blah blah blah! Finally I had to fake a non-existent throat infection and run downstairs for an adhrat waali chai!"

Payal chuckled and Ayush said, "You once told me that this was the reason why chachu and maasi left"

Payal's smile vanished and Ayush said sighing, "I feel so suffocated by this. How would have they felt?"

"That's why they left" Payal whispered and looked away.

Ayush sighed and wrapped an arm around his mother.

"I wish they were here" she whispered, "I couldn't even take my sister's baby in my hands. Hell, I don't even know whether it's a boy or girl. They left just like that! All because of that woman!"

Chapter 2

Raizada Mansion, New Delhi

12.35 am

"You seem to be a night owl!" Akash commented as he walked into the terrace seeing Aisha there.

Aisha turned and smiled, "Aap bhi!"

Akash chuckled and said, "Work pressure!"

Aisha nodded and Akash said, "Waise...I want to apologize for yesterday. I shouldn't have talked like that!"

Aisha frowned and Akash said, "When you came back late..."

"Ah it's fine" Aisha chuckled, "I should've come early!"

"Aisha, it's not like I dislike you. I don't have any problem with you. But yesterday I was really worried. Your phone was off and I didn't know what to do. It was 3 in the morning and I even thought of going to police" Akash said sighing.

"Sorry" she said slowly.

"I don't have any problem with parties and all. I scolded you because it was really late and Delhi isn't safe for girls. If something happens to you, I won't be able to forgive myself. Lavanya has trust in me and I cannot break that trust!" Akash said, "I don't differentiate between you and Ayush"

"Then why do you hate when I call your wife ma?" she asked slowly.

Akash took a deep breath and said, "I know Payal likes it. Even I do. But I lost some very important people of my life because of this ma chakkar. Years back, something similar happened and...." He stopped himself and looked away.

"ASR....Khushi right?" Aisha asked slowly.

"La told you?" Akash asked.

"Not everything but small pieces, here and there....I know that you have a brother and he left the house with his wife and new born baby" Aisha said.

Akash nodded and said, "Me and Payal are the only ones who miss them here. My dadi too....she passed away few years back. And Ayush...he doesn't know much about them. He has never seen them!"

Aisha smiled faintly and Akash said, "I get busy with office and Ayush is busy with his friends. Payal gets very lonely. She doesn't talk much with other people here. And then you came. I've never seen Payal this happy after they left. And I owe you a huge thank you for that!"

Aisha smiled widely and said, "I like her too. Sometimes I miss mamma and I go down to the kitchen where she will be. And then I feel better. That's why I call her ma!"

Akash smiled and Aisha asked, "Didn't they call you? Not even once?"

Akash nodded no, "I tried finding them but they seem to be vanished!" he looked at Aisha and said smiling faintly, "I don't even know whether they had a son or daughter. He or she would've been your age by now! 23!"

"How old is Ayush?" Aisha asked.

"20"

"Hawww....he is younger to me! And he calls me Aisha! That boy better call me didi!" Aisha cried.

Akash chuckled and said, "I'll tell him!"

.

.

.

"Bahot mazaa aya!" Khushi said happily and clapped her hands like a kid. Arnav rolled his eyes and Akash and Payal chuckled. "Ha Khushi ji" NK said cheerfully, "we should often do this. It's so fun!"

"NK bhai you're right" Akash said leaning back on the couch, "It's been a long time right? Remember, before wedding we three used to go out for long drives at night!"

"Ha Akash" NK cried.

"Yeah right!" Arnav scoffed, "More like me being a driver for two drunkards!"

"Drunkards!" Khushi and Payal cried and looked at Akash and NK.

"Err...kabhi kabhi....like very rarely....bhaiiii!!!" Akash cried seeing Payal's glare.

Arnav chuckled.

It was 11 pm in the night and the five were out in the garden sitting around a small camp fire.

"I like it when we spend time like this!" Payal said smiling, "You guys are busy with office and me and Khushi with our dabba service. We should spend moments like this more often!"

"I wish di also joined us!" Khushi said sighing.

Arnav sighed and looked back at the house.

"What should we do bhai?" Akash asked shaking his head, "Di is....she is so depressed after learning Shyam's truth!"

"I think we should give her some time" Payal said.

"It'll be hard for her. She trusted him so much" NK said sighing.

Arnav took a deep breath and said, "She doesn't talk to anyone. Not even to me. Not even to nani. I don't know what to do. She just sits in her room, eat what HP takes to her room and walk around like a corpse."

"I think we should ask di to adopt a child" Khushi said and everyone looked at her, "What hurts her the most is that Shyam, the one whom she loved the most, killed her child. This added to her shock of her child's death. So adopting a child would make her feel better!"

"I don't agree" Akash said shaking his head, "Just because we want her to come out of her depression, we cannot let her adopt a child. I mean, it wouldn't be fair to that child. When he or she grows up, wouldn't they want someone as a father?"

"Yeah, no matter if the whole family stands by her side, no one can be a father!" NK said.

"But I think..." Khushi began when Arnav cut her off, "When a kid is upset, you show them their favorite toy to make them feel better. That's what you're saying here! To bring di back, you are suggesting adopting a child! But Khushi, adopting a child and buying a Barbie doll is different!"

"He is right" Payal said.

"Okay okay" Khushi said chuckling, "It was a suggestion. Now don't eat me up!"

Everyone chuckled and Arnav said, "You're a kid and that's why you have childish suggestions!"

"Hawww" Khushi gasped and smacked his arm.

.

.

"What are you thinking?" Payal asked patting his arm. Akash looked at her and then at the opened laptop before him. "Ah nothing, I was....nothing"

Payal smiled faintly and said, "Arnav ji and Khushi...hai na..."

"NK too!" Akash said chuckling, "When is he coming?"

"It's rakshabandan in two days. He'll be here!" Payal said smiling.

"Ha, after all he has to get a rakhi tied from you" he said smiling.

Payal smiled and nodded.

"I wish my sister was here too..." Akash said smiling sadly and looked at the rakhi she had tied him, years ago.

Payal looked at him and took a deep breath.

"She loved rakshabandans" Akash said smiling at Payal, "She used to demand strange things from me as gifts. Remember when she made me took all of bhai's suits and replace it with colourful shirts?"

Payal chuckled and said, "She knows that you won't agree normally. But on rakshabandan you're bound to grand her wishes right?"

Akash chuckled and nodded.

"I miss them Akash" Payal whispered.

"Me too" Akash whispered.

Chapter 3

Raizada Mansion, New Delhi

10.30 am

"Di" Akash called as he barged into Anjali's room.

Anjali and mami looked up from the bed where they were selecting sarees. "What happened Akash?" Anjali asked.

"You asking me what happened?" Akash asked angrily, "Your credit card bill has come. 35 lakhs, di! What the hell did you do with this much money?"

"Why are you shouting for that?" Anjali cried, "It was my friend's wedding and I bought saree and jewellery for that."

"For 35 lakhs?" Akash cried.

"Hello hi bye bye, diamond jewellery costs that much bitwa!" mami said.

"What's the need for jewellery? You already have tons of it" Akash pointed to her wardrobe.

"So I cannot even buy my favorite jewellery now?" Anjali asked in tears, "How can you account your sister's money Akash?"

"Excuse me" Akash scoffed, "The need for checking accounts arise when your sister spends like a maniac. And what did you say, YOUR money? Please di, we all knows who is earning here!"

"Dekha mami" Anjali said in tears, "Look how he's talking. So I don't have any right in your money?"

"It's not about rights" Akash cried in irritation, "Stop spending like this. Money doesn't grow on trees. If you had spent on some needful situation I would have never questioned. But this, saree and accessories for 35 lakhs! What the fuck!"

"Akash stop" Mami said, "She is your sister. It's her money too!"

Akash groaned, "You guys won't change. Whatever it is, I'm blocking your credit card and I won't be depositing huge amount in your account"

"What?" Anjali cried.

"I should've done this earlier" Akash said shaking his head, "Money is hard earned di. Learn to respect it! If not respecting, at least, don't insult my hardwork!"

"Akash" Mami shouted.

"Now don't make me wash out her account completely" Akash shouted angrily and walked out.

"Akash has changed a lot" Anjali said sadly.

"Ha" mami said, "He is no more our Akash bitwa. Now he's Payal's husband and Ayush's father!"

"They don't even care for Ayush" Anjali said scoffing, "Right from his childhood I was the one who looked after him. Payal was always busy with her stupid dabba business and Akash handling AR. No one cared for the boy. And now, they are pampering him!"

.

.

.

AR Fashions, New Delhi

11.00 am

.

"Why were you late?" Aman asked as Akash sat in his cabin.

"Had a row with di" Akash muttered and said, "Block her credit card and yes, withdraw amount from her account. Only 3000INR should remain in that!"

Aman nodded and said, "Those two students are here. The one week internship is over so their extended internship starts today. I was waiting for you to come so that you can meet them!"

"Oh yes, send them in!" Akash nodded.

Few minutes later, Aman walked in with Aisha and a boy.

"Hey Aisha" Akash said smiling. "Hello unc...sir" Aisha said smiling sheepishly. Akash smiled and stood up. He extended his hand to the boy who smiled and shook it. "Ayan Sharma, sir"

"Akash Singh Raizada. Sit down both of you" he said and both of them sat down.

"So, I liked your designs very much. You guys are extremely talented and I'm glad that you accepted our proposal to work for us for one month! If you prove to be good as I think you are, I'm gonna offer you job here, which you can join after graduation"

"Thank you sir" Ayan said and Aisha nodded, "We'll work hard"

Akash smiled and nodded. "We've an upcoming show based on traditional wear. Half of the designs are complete. First I want you to help our designers in finishing up the designed ones. You would get to know more about the theme and our company through this. And then you'll be asked to submit your own designs!"

Both of them nodded and Akash dialed for Aman.

"Aman will take you to the head designer. She will assign you to her subordinates. They'll explain your works better" he said.

They both nodded and stood up. "Thank you sir!"

They were about to turn when Akash called Aisha. Ayan walked out of the cabin and Aisha turned to Akash.

"Payal has sent you tiffin" Akash said smiling and forwarded her tiffin.

"Awww" Aisha cried and grabbed the tiffin.

"Is he the one?" Akash asked raising his eyebrow.

"Who?" she asked frowning.

"Ayan. The one with whom you go out. I've heard you and Payal talking about him!"

Aisha blushed and bit her tongue. "Ha..."

"Aww look at your face!" Akash chuckled, "Go...Aman must be waiting"

.

.

.

"So yummy" Ayan said tasting Aisha's food.

"Ma cooked it" Aisha said smiling.

Ayan hummed and said pouting "All I have here is a pizza"

"Aww...I'll ask ma to pack you a tiffin as well!" Aisha said chuckling.

"Will she?" he asked happily.

"Let me ask. She owns a dabba service so packing another tiffin won't be a huge task for her"

"Haa" Ayan said, "Waise I don't like you staying there. Why don't you stay in a hostel?"

"Why? I like it there" she said smiling.

"But do you have freedom there?" he asked chuckling.

"As far as I ignore Anjali aunty and Manorama aunty, I've enough freedom there!" she said.

"Aur Ayush?" he asked raising an eyebrow.

She stopped eating and said smirking, "So that's it? Freedom and all was just an excuse. You're jealous of Ayush!"

"What! Jealous and me? No way!" he scoffed.

"Ayan is jealous" Aisha sang, "Don't worry. Ayush is younger to me. Chota bhai he!"

Ayan hid his smile and looked away.

"Waise do you have enough facilities at your PG?" she asked.

"Ha..." he said, "I do find it a bit difficult but...PG is affordable. I mean, fee at NIFT is huge and I don't want to burden papa and mamma with hostel dues. Here it's fine. Low rent and food is free too."

.

.

Aman walked into his cabin and Akash looked up.

He forwarded few files and said, "Needed your signatures!"

Akash nodded and took his pen.

"Those kids are amazing" Aman said and Akash smiled.

"I mean...totally amazing. Aisha is good but that boy...man....he is rocking! I saw him helping Rashid to finish a saree. Brilliant ideas and perfect color combinations! The saree looked magnificent by the end!"

"Achaa" Akash said and looked at him.

"Ha yaar....and...I don't if I feel coz I miss him a lot...but that boy reminds me a lot of ASR. That look he has when he concentrates and...trust me, when you see him from back, you see ASR!" Aman cried.

Akash nodded and Aman looked out of the glass window. "Ah there he is in the cafeteria. Facing us backwards. Look look!"

Akash stood up and looked down through the glass door. The boy dressed up in a blue jeans and maroon shirt was facing them backwards.

Aman was indeed right.

If Aman hadn't told him that it's Ayan, Akash would've definitely mistaken him for his brother.

Chapter 4

Raizada Mansion, New Delhi

4.30 pm

.

Aisha chuckled and Ayush groaned as NK chachu went on exposing his childhood secrets.

"Chachu please" Ayush cried.

Payal smiled as she walked into the living room with chai and pakodas.

"Hello hi bye bye...pakodas!" mami cried as she penguin-walked to the living room with Anjali following her.

They sat on the couch opposite to NK and Ayush.

"How was your college Ayush?" Anjali asked smiling.

"As usual bua!" Ayush said and took a bite on the pakoda.

Payal sat next to Aisha on the adjacent couch and handed her the tea.

"How was your day?" she asked to her.

"Great. AR is awesome!" Aisha said happily.

"What are you doing at AR?" Anjali asked sharply.

"She works as an intern there" NK answered for her, "You live in this house na? And you didn't know. Even I, the one who came today, knows this!"

"Who considers me as a member of this family?" Anjali said sadly and looked down.

Ayush looked at Payal who rolled her eyes. NK hid his laughter and shook his head. Some people never change.

"It's been a year that you're here chachu. You're staying for a month right?" Ayush asked.

"Nahi yaar, just a few days!" NK said apologetically.

"And you'll be coming next year only? For rakshabandan!" Ayush said.

NK nodded and Ayush groaned.

"NK bhai" Payal cried, "Why don't you visit us often!"

NK shrugged and said, "You know I don't like coming here"

"Ouch that hurts!" Ayush muttered.

"I didn't mean you champ. You know what I meant" NK patted his arm and looked at Anjali and mami.

Payal looked at Aisha and said, "Tomorrow we'll be having a small pooja here as its rakshabandan. You can invite your friends if you want!"

"Pooja he party nahi" Anjali scoffed.

"So?" Payal raised an eyebrow, "You called all of your kitty party friends for nani's barsi. So keep quiet!"

Aisha smiled and said, "I'll call Ayan"

"Ha I wanna meet him" Ayush said smiling.

"Ayan who?" mami asked sharpening her ears.

"Her boyfriend dadi" Ayush said.

"Acha...he is in your class?" Anjali asked.

Aisha nodded her head.

"College romance" NK sang, "Not bad"

She smiled and Anjali asked, "Does your mother know about this?"

"No" Aisha mumbled.

"Hello hi bye bye, we should inform Lavanya that her daughter is roaming around with boys instead of studying!"

Payal rolled her eyes and said, "Not with boys but with one boy. And it's her boyfriend. So why don't you concentrate on your make up and stay quiet?"

Ayush and NK hid their laughter and looked at Payal. You go ma/Payal bhabhi.

"Invite him" NK said, "Even I want to meet this beautiful girl's boyfriend"

"Advance main warning: Ayush, he is jealous of you!" Aisha said chuckling.

"Me? Why?" Ayush frowned.

"Arrey" Anjali said, "Of course he would be jealous of you beta. You're the Raizada heir! How can anyone not wish to be like you?"

Payal glared at her and NK said rolling his eyes, "Are you this stupid or are you acting?" he turned to Aisha and asked, "Why is he jealous of our Ayush beta!"

"Coz I stay here and he's scared whether I'll fall in love with you!" Aisha said.

Ayush burst out laughing and so did Payal and NK. "You and me! Arrey we're bhai behen!"

.

.

.

"Nanhe ji" Khushi whispered as she peeked into NK's room. NK looked up from his laptop and found Khushi near the door.

"Kya huva Khushi ji?" he asked stepping out of the bed. Khushi entered the room and closed the door.

"Listen to me" she whispered.

He frowned and nodded.

"Woh I want to surprise Arnav ji. Help me!" she whispered.

"Okay, we'll hide behind the door and jump out screaming when he comes" he said.

"Uffo" Khushi said, "I said surprise not scare him to death!"

"What is surprise for? It's his birthday?" NK frowned.

"Nahi"

"Your birthday?"

"Nahi"

"Then? Are you pregnant?"

Not getting an answer he looked at her with widened eyes. "Khushi ji! You're...."

"Sshhhh" Khushi hushed and said, "No one knows. I wanted to tell Arnav ji first! And you spoiled it!"

"Nahi nahi nahi...I don't know I don't know....I've forgotten it. Erase it" NK said and wiped his hands in air as if he's erasing his memory.

Khushi giggled and NK hugged her, "Congratulations bhabhi!"

Khushi looked at him surprised, "You've never called me bhabhi!"

"Now I did! Oh my god....I'm gonna be an uncle! What! NO way! I'm not that old...forget it...you're gonna have a baby! Chotte's chotte is on the way! WOW! I mean....oh my god...."

"Nanhe ji relax" Khushi said giggling.

"Arrey how can I relax! We've to plan the surprise. We've to reveal it like a dhamaka! Nannav should be shocked and frozen and dumbstruck and....whatever...come LET'S PLAN!"

.

NK took a deep breath. Sitting on the green recliner, he took a look of the room. Payal made sure that the room remains intact, just as they left it. Not a spot of dust to be spotted, not a thing moved from its place, no one would say that the owners of this room had left it for 23 years. He smiled at the wardrobe full of their clothes, the dressing table with her accessories, the cupboard full of files....everything reminded of them. His eyes fell on the wooden crib and a faint smile appeared on his face.

.

"What are you doing? Where are you taking us?" Arnav cried as Akash covered his eyes and made him walk while NK had Khushi's eyes covered.

"Be careful with her dammit" Arnav shouted.

"Bhai, NK bhai and Payal are with her" Akash said rolling his eyes.

"Ha Nannav you just walk" NK said chuckling.

They entered the room and took their hands off.

"Why is it dark here?" Khushi asked looking around the dark room.

"Switch on the lights idiots" Arnav said.

"Shoo relax" Payal said giggling and switched on the lights.

"Okay, now tell us why you have brought us here and..." Arnav stopped his rant when his eyes spotted on something. Khushi followed his gaze and gasped. She covered her mouth with her palm and looked at the three who were smiling.

Arnav held Khushi's hand and both of them walked to the wooden crib decorated with flowers.

"Yeh...this..." Arnav stammered and looked at the trio.

"This is for our nannav's and Khushi ji's chottu!" NK said smiling and wrapped an arm around Akash.

"It's our selection. Did you like it?" Akash asked smiling.

"Like it? It's amazing" Khushi whispered and ran her fingers through the crib.

"It's so beautiful" Arnav said smiling widely.

"Ha it'll be more beautiful when someone lies in there" Payal said caressing Khushi's 7 months belly.

Suddenly Khushi gasped and Payal chuckled, "Ah see...the baby likes it!"

"He's playing football in there I guess" Akash said chuckling.

"How do you know it's a he?" NK asked raising his eyebrow.

"It'll be a he" Akash said stubbornly.

"It'll be a girl. A princess" NK said.

"Boy"

"Girl"

"Boy"

"Girl"

"Why don't you ask the doctor to reveal the gender?" Payal asked.

"Nahi" Khushi said, "I don't want to know it now. I want to know it after his or her birth!"

"Ha" Arnav said nodding.

"Let's bet" Akash said.

"Fine. 1000 bucks!" NK said and shook hands with Akash.

.

NK wiped his eyes and walked to the bedside table. Taking the frame he looked at the pic taken at their wedding. Smiling sadly he whispered, "Where are you guys? I miss you so much!"

"Uncle"

He turned hearing a voice. "Ma is calling you for dinner" Aisha said.

NK nodded and Aisha frowned, "Are you okay?"

NK hummed and kept the frame back.

"Is this your room? From the day I came here it's been locked" Aisha said entering the room and looking around.

"No, it's my brother's room" NK said slowly.

Aisha nodded and her eyes fell on the photoframe. "This..." she whispered.

NK took the frame and said, "This is my brother and his wife. Nannav...I mean Arnav and Khushi...."

"But uncle this....this is Ayan's parents" Aisha whispered.

NK looked at her shocked.

Chapter 5

Raizada Mansion, New Delhi

9.30 am

.

"So this is Ayan huh?" Payal asked smiling. Aisha nodded and Ayan bend down to take her blessings.

"Hey jeeju" Ayush said hugging him.

"Jeeju?" Ayan asked surprised.

"Ha, Aisha is my di so you're my jeeju" Ayush said laughing, "Now stop being jealous of me. I won't steal your girl!"

Ayan gaped and looked at Aisha who looked at the ceiling. "I'm not jealous of you....why would I be jealous" Ayan cried shrugging.

"Don't play Ayan, Aisha told us everything" Payal said chuckling. Ayan smiled sheepishly and looked away.

"Ayan this is NK" Aisha said slowly as NK walked into the hall.

NK looked at Aisha and then at Ayan. NK smiled and hugged him tight.

Ayan was taken aback but hugged him back.

"I'm NK" NK said slowly.

"Hello uncle" Ayan said smiling.

"Ah no uncle....I told Aisha too...makes me feel old. Call me NK!"

"Okay...NK" Ayan said smiling.

"Hello hi bye bye, is this your boyfriend?" mami asked walking into the hall.

"Namaste" Ayan folded his hands. Mami said, "I'm Manorama, eldest in the house!"

"Hello, I'm Anjali. I'm Ayush's..."

"Bua" Ayush completed.

Ayan smiled and folded his hands.

"Chalo pooja karthe he" Payal called out and Ayan looked around, "Where is Akash sir?"

"He'll come now. He has to make an important call" NK said. Ayan nodded and followed" Payal while Aisha stayed behind.

"Did you tell him anything?" NK whispered.

"No" she whispered, "And you? Ma and Akash uncle?"

"Nahi...I haven't told anyone. I have to confirm" NK whispered and Aisha nodded.

"Where are you from Ayan?" NK asked as the whole family sat in the living room couch after the pooja and rakhi tying.

"Shimla"

"Do you have any siblings?" Payal asked.

"Ha...choti behen. Amara" Ayan said.

"Then why didn't you go home for rakshabandan?" Anjali asked surprised.

"Woh she is having her board exams and papa has banished me from entering the house" Ayan said smiling, "If I'm home then she would spend the whole day following me everywhere!"

Everyone chuckled and mami said, "Hello hi bye bye, but it's rakshabandan. She has to tie you rakhi!"

"Rakhi isn't important than her exams, right?" Ayan said smiling, "I just want her to perform well in exams. Papa and ma too"

"Ha that's true" Payal said smiling.

"But still" Anjali said shaking her head, "Rakhi is important. A sister ties it to her brother and the brother promises her to take care of her for a lifetime. To be with her for every sadness. Rakhi is a symbol of love between brother and sister!"

Akash coughed and NK rolled his eyes. Payal looked at the ceiling. "Look who is talking" she muttered under her breath.

Ayan chuckled and said, "I don't need a rakhi to know how much sister loves me! And promises...why should I even promise that I will take care of her? I will be there for her and she knows that!"

"Ayan, what does your parents do?" Payal asked changing the topic.

"Papa has a tailoring shop. He is a very good designer and people in our village get their clothes done from him. And we've converted a section of our house as a restaurant. So mamma looks after that" Ayan said.

Anjali chuckled and said, "You know that Aisha's mother Lavanya is a fashion designer and her father Karan owns a financial company, right?"

Ayan looked at Aisha and then at Anjali. "Ha yes" he said slowly.

"Hello hi bye bye you think her parents would agree to marry off their daughter to a village boy?" Mami asked laughing.

"Exactly" Anjali said shaking her head, "Her father owns a financial company and yours....a tailor?"

"Stop it bua" Ayush whispered.

"What does your father do?" Akash asked sharply at Anjali.

Anjali gulped and said, "My matter is different"

"Why? Just because...." Payal began when Ayan cut her off, "It's okay aunty...it's fine...please stop"

"Anjali aunty" Aisha said calmly, "You don't have to worry about me. I don't know what decision my parents will take regarding Ayan but I'm sure that they won't reject him because of his parents' occupation. And plus what's wrong in being a tailor? When a tailor sits in a well maintained cabin, under AC, in a huge building, you call him a fashion designer. That's all!"

Akash chuckled and nodded, "Remember di, bhai started AR like that. He used to stitch clothes of his own before we hired employees!"

"Whatever" Anjali muttered and walked away. Mami followed her.

"I'm so sorry Ayan" Akash said with a fallen face, "I....I never thought she would..."

"It's fine" Ayan said slowly.

Aisha looked at NK who was not taking his eyes off Ayan.

"Aisha you take him around. I'll come now" Akash said and stood up when his phone rang.

Payal and Ayush too left for some work, leaving Aisha, Ayan and NK in the living room.

Aisha looked at NK who asked, "So Ayan, you're from Shimla? I mean, your parents are also from Shimla?"

"Yeah, we've been at Shimla for a very long time. And yes they are also from Shimla" Ayan said.

"What are their names?" NK asked.

"My parents?"

NK nodded.

"It's Ar...sorry my phone..." Ayan said and grabbed his ringing phone from his pocket. "It's my sister. Excuse me" he stood up and walked away.

"So?" Aisha whispered.

"It's him" NK whispered, "I'm sure. Are you sure that you have seen Nannav and Khushi ji in his family photo"

"Yes, damn sure. It's them"

NK nodded and whispered smilingly, "Akash won the bet. It's a boy!"

Aisha smiled faintly.

"But as far as you have told me, ASR is a powerful person. Born to be a boss. Why is he staying a low life?" Aisha whispered.

"Whatever he does, he makes sure that he reaches the peak of success" NK whispered, "But....I don't know why he chose a low life. Have Ayan ever told you about any financial difficulties?"

"He is studying under educational loan. And he stays in PG because hostel fee is huge" Aisha said.

NK nodded and Ayan came back. "Ah so, my parents name is Arnav and Khushi"

"Oh" NK said calmly, while he was dancing inside, "So Sharma? Dad's surname?"

"Nahi...dad's surname is Raizada. I think Sharma is...ah I don't know. I never asked"

"Raizada?" NK asked, "Even this a Raizada family!"

"Yeah I know. There are so many families with same name na? Actually there are three Ayan Sharmas in my class" Ayan said chuckling.

"So you dad's and mom's family doesn't stay with you?"

"Dad's family used to stay with us. Dadu and dadi. But they passed away few years ago" Ayan said smiling.

NK frowned but nodded smiling.

.

"Thank you inviting me" Ayan said smiling, "I had a great time"

Payal and Akash nodded smiling and Anjali rolled her eyes.

"I should take lea...." He couldn't complete when a voice rang in the house, "SURPRISE!"

Everyone turned and Aisha squealed, "Mamma?" she ran and hugged Lavanya tight. "Aap yahan?" she cried.

"Well I thought to visit you. How are you dear?" Lavanya asked cupping her face. "Great" Aisha said smiling.

"Hey Lavanya" Payal said and hugged her. Akash too hugged her.

"NK? When did you...ah it's rakshabandan" Lavanya said and hugged NK.

"Hello di, hello mami ji" Lavanya said and turned to Ayush. "Hey Ayush" "Hello aunty"

"Who is this? Your friend?" she asked looking at Ayan.

"Err..." Ayush stammered when mami said, "Hello hi bye bye, why don't you ask your daughter who he is!"

Lavanya frowned and looked at Aisha who stood pale.

"Mamma...he is my friend" she said slowly.

"Why are you sweating for that?" Lavanya asked chuckling and turned to Ayan. "What's your name?"

"Ayan" he said slowly.

"Friend?" Anjali scoffed, "Yeah right. The friend whom she introduced to us as her boyfriend. The friend with whom she stays out at night! Aisha, do you do this with all your friends? I wonder how many friends you have."

Chapter 6

.

"Friend?" Anjali scoffed, "Yeah right. The friend whom she introduced to us as her boyfriend. The friend with whom she stays out at night! Aisha, do you do this with all your friends? I wonder how many friends you have."

"Stop it" Ayan shouted, "Aap kuch bhi bolti ja rahi ho!"

"Lavanya" Mami said, "you better control your daughter. She walks into the house at 3 am in the morning after partying with this boy!"

"Ha and on top of that...." Anjali began when Lavanya said calmly, "Enough"

Everyone looked at her. Lavanya took a deep breath and said sternly, "You cannot call my daughter characterless...and that too in front of me? Not happening"

"Arrey nahi Lavanya" Anjali said hurriedly, "We didn't say that!"

"But you meant that" Lavanya said sharply and looked at Aisha who was in tears. Then she looked at Ayan who stood not knowing what to do.

"Ayan right?" she asked and he nodded.

"I've taken a long flight to here and am very tired. We'll meet you later!" she said and extended her palm. Ayan shook hands with her and Lavanya looked at Ayush, "Ayush walk him out"

Ayush nodded and Ayan followed him out.

Lavanya looked at Aisha and said, "We'll talk later. Let me freshen up"

"You're accepting them?" Anjali cried.

"That's my decision to take, not yours" Lavanya said angrily, "And why are you getting hyper? What's wrong if she has a boyfriend? Bacche he...it's their age to fall in love. When I was of her age, your brother was my boyfriend. Remember?"

Anjali began to say something when Lavanya said, "She is my daughter. I know how to talk to her and what decisions to make regarding her. And on this matter, I will talk to her, not you. She doesn't have to clear her stand before you di"

"Well she lives here!" Anjali said crossing her arms.

"That doesn't make her your daughter" Lavanya said angrily, "Fine then," she looked at Aisha, "Pack your bags. I'll get you admitted to college hostel"

"La no" Payal cried.

"I'm sorry Payal" Lavanya said shaking her head, "I thought she would be happy here and won't miss her family. But this...I cannot let my daughter stay at a place where people question her character"

"La please" Payal said in tears, "I promise you, nothing of this sort will happen again. But please don't take her away. Please."

Lavanya sighed and said, "I need to take rest. I'm having a splitting headache"

.

.

.

.

"I don't know NK" Lavanya said sighing, "I've to talk to Karan as well. We don't know anything about that boy. Just his name. Ayan Sharma"

NK smiled and said, "I know more about him"

Lavanya looked at him and NK asked, "Do you know who his parents are?"

She nodded no and NK took out his mobile showing her the pic Aisha forwarded him in whataspp.

"Oh my god" she whispered and snatched his mobile. Gazing at the phone she looked at him in tears. NK smiled and nodded.

"ASR and chamkili..." Lavanya whispered, "Ayan is their son?"

He nodded and said, "Ayan doesn't know that this is his father's family. They are in Shimla right from his childhood and he believes his family hails from there."

"Did you meet them?" she asked.

"No. I came to know this yesterday. I haven't told Akash and Payal bhabhi. But how will we meet them? We don't know where they are in Shimla and we cannot go and ask the boy where his parents live. I mean what will we answer him?" NK said.

"So what are you planning to do?"

"I will bring them here. In this house" NK said determined, "I'm not leaving without meeting nannav and Khushi ji" he looked at Lavanya and said, "And for that, I need your help"

Lavanya looked at him and asked, "What help?"

"You see your daughter is in relationship with their son. Ask Ayan to bring his parents to Delhi so that you can meet them" he said.

Lavanya thought for a second and nodded, "I'll do that"

NK smiled and said, "Thanks"

Lavanya smiled and said, "A part of my tension is cleared" NK looked at her and she said, "Ayan is their son. ASR and chamkili...I can always trust my daughter with them. And Ayan...I just need to know more about the boy and then I'll be perfectly okay with this relationship"

"Destiny right?" NK said smiling, "Out of all boys in her college Aisha fell in love with our nannav's and Khushi ji's son!"

Lavanya chuckled and nodded.

Payal walked to them with a tray of kheer and both of them ended their conversation.

"Why are you sad?" Lavanya asked, "Listen Payal, I'm not taking Aisha anywhere. Don't be sad"

"Nahi it's..." Payal said sitting next to them, "Seeing Ayan, I don't know why, but he reminded a lot of Arnav ji and Khushi"

Lavanya looked at NK.

"He looks a lot like Arnav ji. And his smile is exactly like Khushi!" Payal said sadly, "God I'm thinking too much about them that I see them in every person I meet!"

Don't worry Payal bhabhi, NK said to himself, soon you're gonna meet them. I promise you that.

.

.

.

"Everything became alright na?" Khushi asked smiling and leaned on Arnav's shoulder. Arnav wrapped his arm around her shoulder and hummed.

"Di has come out of her shell" NK said smiling.

"She treats me like a queen" Khushi said giggling, "Takes care of me and my baby"

Arnav cleared his throat and said, "Our baby"

"Ha wahi" Khushi said chuckling.

Payal nodded and said, "Di is so happy now. Dekho na, just the mention of a child brought happiness in this house. Now imagine how Shantivan will be when he or she comes."

"I'm so excited" Akash said happily, "I'm gonna be a chachu"

"And I'll make sure that the baby calls you Akki" NK said smirking.

"What?" Akash said his eyes widening.

"Akki" everyone giggled.

"No way. NK NOOOO" Akash cried.

"I don't know about Akash but I'm not gonna let my child call you NK" Arnav said smirking, "My baby will take revenge on you for calling me nannav"

NK sat mortified and Akash laughed at his face.

"Bhai, we should make the baby call him nandkishore" Akash said.

"Nahi nandu chachu" Payal said.

"Nanhe chachu" Khushi said.

"STOP IT" NK shouted, "Your child better call me NK"

"NO WAY" everyone shouted.

"Arrey why are you shouting?" Anjali asked coming to the living room, "Don't you know that it's harmful for the baby. Khushi ji come here"

"Sorry" everyone said slowly. Anjali helped Khushi stand up and said, "Khushi ji you have to take care of yourself. You have a life growing inside you! Arrey you still act like a kid"

Khushi pouted and said, "Sorry di"

"She is a kid" Arnav commented and Khushi glared at him.

"Chalo, let me take you upstairs. Do you need something? Juice or any-thing?"

"Nahi di, I'm fine" Khushi said and Anjali held her shoulders helping her to walk.

Akash took a deep breath and looked to the dining room where Anjali was hovering around Ayush to eat.

"Bas bua, I'm full" Ayush whined.

"Arrey aise kaise...have one more paratha" she said.

"Nahi...." Ayush said.

"Come I'll feed you"

"Nahi nahi, I'll eat myself" Ayush said and tore the paratha.

Anjali smiled and caressed his hair.

Akash shook his head and looked away. You really need counseling di. Your obsession to be a mother made us lose bhai and Khushi. He said to himself.

Chapter 7

"Uffo di" Akash said shaking his head, "Relax. Bhai is with Khushi na"

"But Akash..." Anjali said worriedly.

"Di, concentrate on the movie" NK whispered his eyes fixed on the action movie playing on the screen.

Akash, Payal, NK and Anjali had gone out for a movie. Khushi who was in her 8 and half month of pregnancy was ordered to take rest and Arnav stayed by her side.

"I'm so worried" Anjali whispered.

"Nothing will happen to Khushi" Payal said.

"Not about her. About the baby" Anjali said shaking her head.

Payal looked at her and hummed.

"I hope the baby is fine" Anjali muttered, "Khushi ji doesn't know how to take care. She never takes rest and...."

"Di, Khushi is a mother. She loves and takes care of her child more than anyone" Payal whispered, "We don't have to worry about it"

Anjali was about to say something when Payal's phone rang.

Arnav ji calling.

"Ha Arnav ji" Payal said, "What? Oh okay...okay relax....we're coming. I have packed her bag and kept it under your bed. Take it and take her to city hospital. I'll inform the doctor."

Everyone looked at her. "Khushi ji started to have pain?" Anjali gasped.

"Arnav ji...Arnav ji relax" Payal said standing up. She looked at others and said, "Let's go"

"Arnav ji relax....take care of her...don't worry. It's gonna be alright. We're here na..." she said and everyone rushed to the car.

"Akash drive fast. Arnav ji is so worried. It seems like he's having the labour pain not Khushi" Payal said shaking her head.

.

.

.

"Congratulations. Baby and mother are perfectly fine. The nurse have taken the baby to take weight" doctor said and walked away.

"Arrey...doctor....doctor saab...." Everyone called out but he walked away to another operation room.

"He seems busy" NK said chuckling.

"Idiot. He didn't tell the gender" Arnav cried.

"Ha yaar" Akash face palmed.

"Chalo we'll wait for the nurse" Payal said shaking her head.

"What the" Arnav muttered irritated, "My baby is born. Nurse took the baby for taking weight and I don't even know whether it's a boy or girl!"

"You waited 8 months right? Now wait for just 8 minutes" NK said patting his shoulder.

"Chotte" Anjali called out and Arnav looked at her smiling.

He hugged her and said, "Di, I'm a father now!" he withdrew the hug and smiled through tears, "I have a baby..."

Anjali looked down and nodded.

"Kya hua di?" he asked.

"Woh..."

"Di you want to ask me something?" Arnav asked frowning. Everyone looked at them and Anjali nodded.

"Ask me na"

"Whatever I ask, will you give me?" Anjali asked cupping his face.

"Is that even a question? Aap poocho" Arnav asked smiling, "You want to name my baby na? Of course you can!"

"Nahi..."

"Then?"

"Can you give me your baby?" Anjali asked smiling.

And that's where the hell and heaven broke loose.

.

NK sat up on his chair and rubbed his face with his palm. No matter how much years pass by, he can never forget his brother's face when his sister asked him that question.

Can you give me your baby?

How easily did she ask that question! A whole family waiting eagerly for the baby's arrival, Arnav and Khushi's happiness that tripled by her pregnancy, how they cared and loved their unborn child...she didn't even think about anything. With no tinge of regret or shame, with a smiling face, she asked it on his face.

NK gulped down a glass of water.

Only he knows how much he, Akash and Payal suffered without them. After revealing Shyam's truth, they five had become so close. So close that every day they used to spend time together. That masti, those heart-to-heart talks, the late night drives....everything was gone.

They were gone. Without even telling them. Without even revealing whether they had a son or a daughter.

Well now he knows.

It's a son.

Actually it's a son and a daughter! NK smiled.

"Akash, we both won the bet" he whispered.

He did feel guilty for hiding it from Akash and Payal but that was needed. If he tell them then Payal would demand to see Khushi right away. That would mean revealing everything to Ayan.

'If Nannav chose to hid his life from his children, then it's not our place to reveal it. Nannav should do it himself' NK said to himself.

He took out his mobile and started gazing at the pic Aisha sent him. From the moment she sent him, he couldn't take his eyes off it.

There was his nannav standing next to Khushi ji. Nannav's one arm hugging a beautiful young girl by her shoulder and other arm around Khushi's shoulder and Khushi ji leaning her head to meet her son's who was hugging her sideways.

"Your little world" NK whispered, "I'm happy that you're happy"

His eyes fell on the girl and said, "Amara...matlab beloved..." he smiled and said, "The princess of the family"

"NK" Lavanya said entering the room.

NK looked at her and Lavanya sat before him.

"I met him. Ayan" La said.

"And?"

"Gosh that boy was so nervous" Lavanya chuckled, "Even Aisha was. I was enjoying seeing their faces. I literally acted like those wicked mother-in-laws in saas-bahu serials and Ayan's face was worth watching. He was like...oh shit where have I landed myself!"

NK chuckled and Lavanya said, "Ek baat tho hai...that facial reactions. Exactly like ASR. You know that clueless face of ASR whenever Khushi used to do her nautanki before him? The same face!"

"Did you tell him?"

"Yeah I asked him to make me meet his parents. Bring them to Marriot restaurant before I leave, that's in two days!" Lavanya said.

"Marriot? But why not here?" NK frowned.

"Oh duffer, you think they'll come here?" Lavanya asked smacking his arm.

NK nodded and said, "Ha you're right"

"I can't wait!" Lavanya squealed, "Ayan said he'll call me tonight after he informs his parents. I think he is nervous about it. Telling his parents!"

"Nannav and Khushi ji aren't the types who would disagree to their son's relationship" NK said.

"I don't know about ASR but Khushi would surely never disagree. She would be jumping around for getting a bahu!"

NK laughed and said, "Did you talk to Karan?"

"Yeah, he was like okay. He said, know more about Ayan. His family is okay for him but you know ladka bhi tho acha honi chahiye" Lavanya said, "But I loved the boy. Gosh I enjoyed it today. You should've been there. It was hilarious. I asked him "Why do you love my daughter?" in such a sharp and steel voice that both Ayan and Aisha got pale. He was sweating and said, "woh...I...like her...I love her..." oh my god! At beginning he was really nervous but later he melted and started talking from his heart. I am so impressed!"

Suddenly La's phone rang and she took it, "Ha Ayan tell me"

NK sat up hearing Ayan's name.

"Oh is it? Thank you, yeah I'll be there. Okay...I'll make reservation at the restaurant. Call me when you reach!" she kept the phone and NK looked at her eagerly.

"Tomorrow! Evening! 4.30 pm" Lavanya whispered excitedly.

"YES!" NK cried punching his hand in air.

"What about Akash and Payal?" NK asked.

"We should take them too" La said, "Me, you, Aisha, Akash and Payal"

"Call at Marriot and make a reservation. A secluded corner" NK said and La nodded.

"Wait" NK said, "Make the reservation in your husband's name. Karan Shrivastav" La nodded and took out her phone.

NK looked at the clock that read the time as 11.35 pm.

"18 hours to go! I wish time flew" NK whispered and leaned back on his chair.

Chapter 8

"Have you gone mad di?" Arnav shouted, "You want me to give you my child?"

"Chotte" Anjali said in tears, "I want my baccha chotte. I cannot live without..."

"It's not your baccha...it's my child" Arnav cried, "Mine and Khushi's child. Have you lost it di?"

"You promised to give me anything that I ask"

"My child is not a thing" Arnav shouted, "It's not a toy that I can give you to make you feel better. What made you think that I would do this for you? I never expected this from you di"

"I'm your di. Can't you do such a small thing for me?" she cried.

"Small thing?" Arnav cried, "Is this a small thing? You're asking me to give you MY LIFE! My family! Di, it's my baby you're asking for. Mine and Khushi's symbol of love. You think you can take that away from me?"

"What's happening here?" Nani and mami asked as they walked to them, "Chotte how is Khushi bitiya?"

"She is fine and the baby is also fine. But nani, let's fix the issue that's here" Arnav said angrily.

"What issue?"

"Ask your beloved Anjali bitiya" Arnav said and looked away.

"What wrong did I ask?" Anjali asked angrily. She turned to nani and mami and said, "Nani, mami, I lost my rajkumari because of Khushi ji. So I asked chotte to give me their child. What wrong did I do?"

"Woah woah stop there" Arnav cried, "What do you mean by you lost your rajkumari because of Khushi? What did Khushi do?"

"Di, you lost your princess because of your husband, not because of Khushi ji" NK said angrily.

"If Khushi ji hadn't come into our lives then Shyam ji wouldn't have betrayed me. He would have still loved me. We would have been a happy family. My rajkumari would have been alive!" Anjali cried.

"Anjali bitiya have you gone mad?" Nani cried in disbelief.

"She is right sasumma" mami said shaking her head, "Anjali bitiya is saying the truth. If the Gupta sisters hadn't come into our lives then our family would've been happier. Woh phatti sadi destroyed Anjali bitiya's happiness. So she should give her child to Anjali bitiya"

"Mami aap bhi" Arnav whispered.

"Manorama" Nani shouted, "You've gone mad. And Anjali bitiya, this topic must end NOW!"

"Nahi" Anjali cried, "Woh baccha....Khushi ji won't keep the child safe. She doesn't know how to care and love a baby. Only I know. During her pregnancy I was the one who took care of the baby. The baby loves me not her!"

"So this was why you were taking care of her" Arnav said shaking his head angrily, "Not because you care for her, but because you wanted the child"

"And what did you say, only you know how to take care of a child?" Payal scoffed, "Says the woman who wanted to abort her child. Remember? Arnav ji had to rush in to stop you!"

"You khoon bhari tang shut up" mami shouted.

"No, today I won't" Payal said angrily, "And you better call me Payal hereafter. I'm not your doormat. And you" she turned to Anjali, "Don't even think about coming closer to my sister or her baby. I'll skin you alive!"

"I want that child! It's my baby! My rajkumari!" Anjali cried.

"Fine then" Arnav said crossing his arms, "You're saying it for so long. My baby! My child! Tell me whether it's a boy or girl"

Anjali looked at him and Arnav said scoffing, "We don't even know the gender of the child. You lost your rajkumari? My baby could be a boy. Ab kya rajkumar chahiye?"

"It's my child chotte" Anjali said in tears, "During pregnancy I felt the kick, the movements..."

"You felt it by placing a hand on my wife's stomach" Arnav cried.

"I can feel my baby" Anjali cried.

"What's happening here?" A nurse came and said angrily, "It's labor ward. Keep quiet"

"Sorry" they apologized and the nurse walked away.

Arnav rubbed his face and looked at nani. "Nani you all go home. Akash, take them home. I'll come with Khushi and the baby"

"Nahi I'll stay here" Anjali said stubbornly, "I want to be the one taking my baby home"

"NK" Arnav called out and said, "Take her home"

"Nahi leave me" Anjali cried as NK and Akash dragged her out of the hospital with nani and mami following them.

"You too go" he said to Payal.

"Nahi, I'll be here" Payal said shaking her head.

"Jao Payal" he said.

"Woh Khushi might need me na and...."

"Payal please....go" he said looking down.

"What happened Arnav ji?" Payal asked worriedly, "Listen don't think over di's words. We won't let her do that to you and Khushi. This baby is yours and no one can snatch him or her from you both"

Arnav nodded and Payal walked away patting his back.

"Payal"

She turned and he said, "Thank you for everything"

She frowned and he said, "Tell this to Akash and NK too. And nani too. That I love you all!"

"Why are you saying me this?"

Arnav shrugged and turned away. Payal frowned and walked away to the car.

Everyone returned home and waited for Arnav and Khushi to return home with the baby. Decorating the whole house and arshi's room, they sat in the living room waiting for their arrival.

But they never came.

.

.

Raizada Mansion, New Delhi

1.30 pm

.

"What should I wear Ayan?" Aisha asked over the phone looking at the heaps of dresses on the bed.

"Clothes"

"Very funny" she muttered, "You're in a safe zone now. Mamma liked you. Now it's my turn to impress your parents. How will I do that? What should I say them?"

"Just answer honestly to everything they ask" Ayan said, "And wear anything. Your usual clothes!"

"Nahi nahi nahi, if your parents see me in frocks or gowns then...no I'll wear churidar!"

"Aisha" Ayan said sternly, "Be yourself. Wear what you usually wear! I love you the way you are. You don't have to someone else just to impress my parents"

"Aww love you" Aisha cooed.

"Okay"

"Okay? Say it back"

"Mood nahi he"

"What? Ayan tu bhi na" Aisha cried and Ayan laughed, "Listen let me hang up. I've reached the hotel where papa and mama are"

"Ha okay...wait...is Amara here?" Aisha asked.

"Ha and she is very excited to meet you. Acha chal rakthe he...bye"

"Bye and you still didn't say it back" she shouted.

"Love you tooooooo" Ayan sang and hung up.

"Duffer" Aisha whispered smiling.

"Wear this" Payal said walking in with a pale pink ankle length gown.

Aisha looked at her gaping and Payal said smiling, "I got it for you. Did you like it?"

"It's amazing. But ma, kya aap bhi...it wasn't needed..."

"Chup. It's an important day" Payal said smiling, "Wear this!" Lavanya walked in and said, "Arrey wah, great selection Payal"

Payal nodded smiling and then said, "Waise Lavanya what is the need of all us going? I mean just you and Aisha are enough na. It's your family matter!"

"Arrey you guys are also family" Lavanya said.

"But still...me Akash and NK...it would be so crowded and Ayan's parents won't like it"

"Of course they will like it. They have to like it. Ma I need your approval as well regarding Ayan and his family" Aisha said, "You better come"

"Exactly. I cannot deal with this alone. I need you guys" Lavanya said, "Karan bhi yaha nahi he...he specifically asked me to take you guys!"

Payal sighed and nodded, "Okay then!"

"4.30 pm! Just few more hours to go" Lavanya whispered to herself.

Chapter 9

Marriot Restaurant, New Delhi

4.50 pm

"I'm so nervous" NK said.

"Why are you nervous?" Akash asked frowning.

"Ha Aisha has to be nervous na?" Payal said and looked at Aisha and Lavanya.

"No I meant..." NK stammered and gulped down a glass of water.

"What happened to you guys?" Payal asked looking at NK and Lavanya who kept on looking at the main door.

"Nahi it's 4.50 and they aren't still here" Aisha said looking at her watch.

"Who comes on right time? Other than us?" Akash groaned, "I cancelled a meeting to be here. They better come!"

"Don't worry Akash. This meeting will be much better than your meeting at AR" Lavanya said smiling.

"Hey you guys are here?"

Everyone looked to their left and saw Ayush.

"Ayush? What are you doing here?" Payal asked frowning.

"I came with my friends. We're about to leave" Ayush said pointing to a group of students, "Ah you guys are here to meet Ayan's parents. Nice"

They nodded and Ayush said, "Waise dad, I'll be late tonight. Party hai!"

"Don't get drunk" Akash warned.

Ayush nodded and Payal said, "And call karthe rahna"

He nodded and NK said, "Enjoy"

Ayush chuckled and said, "Okay sure. Bye" he turned but froze on his tracks. "Chachu and maasi" he whispered, but audible to the people sitting on their chairs.

Everyone heard his whisper and turned their heads to the main door.

Ayan walked to them with a girl next to him looking at the huge restaurant with awe. "Sorry we're late. Wo we got stuck in traffic" Ayan said apologetically.

But no one heard his apology. Their eyes were fixed on the two people who walked into the restaurant looking around the luxurious interiors.

"Papa...here" Ayan called out and they turned to him.

Amara ran to them and dragged them to Ayan, "Chalo na papa...mamma kya kar rahe ho...."

"Bhai" Akash whispered and looked at Payal who sat white as a paper. NK looked at both of them and then at his brother and bhabhi.

"Papa, mamma this is Aisha" Ayan said and Aisha stood up smiling.

"Papa" Ayan called out again patting his father's arm.

Arnav and Khushi heard nothing. They were looking at the people sitting on the table, looking shocked at them.

"Papa" Ayan patted his arm and he jerked. "Aisha"

Aisha bend down to take his and Khushi's blessings. Khushi kept her hand on her head. Aisha smiled at both of them and turned to Lavanya, "This is my mamma"

"Hello ASR" Lavanya said smiling and ran to hug Khushi, "Hello chamkili"

"You guys know each other?" Ayan asked surprised.

"Ha" Lavanya said smiling, "Aisha," she turned to her daughter, "Why don't you take Ayan and Amara to another table. You guys talk!"

"Main bhi" Ayush said and Aisha looked at him, "So party?"

"Not important" Ayush whispered looking at Arnav and Khushi who stood still as poles not knowing how to react.

Ayan looked to and fro between the people frowning and Amara clutched his arm sensing something wrong.

"Ayan chalo" Aisha said pulling his arm. "Hello" she said to Amara, "I'm Aisha"

"I know" Amara said cheekily, "Bhabhi"

"Bhabhi! Not bad" Aisha said chuckling and the four walked to another table over a few distance.

Lavanya looked at Arnav and Khushi and said, "Sit"

Akash jumped from his chair and hugged Arnav tight. "Bhai..." he whispered not able to believe that his brother was right before him. A smiled formed on Arnav's face and he wrapped his arm around his little brother.

"Jiji" Khushi whispered through tears seeing Payal who sat frozen in her sit. "Khushi tum....tum sach main yaha...." Payal whispered and Khushi bend down and hugged her tight.

NK cleared his throat and said, "Just for your information nannav and Khushi ji, even I'm here!"

Arnav and Khushi withdrew from the hugs and chuckled. "Come here you monkey" Arnav said chuckling and NK laughed. He hugged him tight and said, "Missed you so much nannav"

He hugged Khushi and said, "You're grown fat!"

"What?" she cried.

"Fatty" NK said chuckling.

"Nanhe ji" Khushi cried and smacked his arm.

"Chalo let's sit" Lavanya said and made Arnav and Khushi sit.

"Waise, you guys can say a thank you to me and Lavanya for our excellent plan to bring Nannav and Khushi ji here!" NK said lifting his collar.

"Plan?" Payal asked.

"Aisha saw your pictures in NK's room" La said looking at Arshi, "And she told us that this is Ayan's parents. So I asked Ayan to bring his parents here so that I can meet them and discuss about their relationship"

"So Aisha is your daughter?" Khushi asked and Lavanya nodded.

"And Aisha and Ayan...." Arnav said and Lavanya nodded and said chuckling, "We're soon to be in-laws!"

Arnav said, "Wo ladka...what's his name?"

"Ayush?" Akash asked.

"Ha...your son?" Khushi asked looking over to the table where Ayush and Ayan were laughing at Amara over something and Aisha cocooning the girl.

"Yes" Payal whispered. Khushi smiled faintly and looked at the kids.

"You have changed a lot" NK said slowly.

"Ha" Lavany said looking at Arnav's pale blue shirt and black pants and Khushi's grey sari with a black blouse, "So simple and...where's the ASR who wore nothing except suits"

"I'm not ASR now Lavanya. I'm just Arnav" Arnav said smiling.

"Where were you guys for all these years?" Akash asked, with a tinge of anger, "We searched and searched but...not sign of you guys at all. Why didn't you guys come back? I know di hurt you a lot but what about us? Didn't you, even for a second, think about us? Just one word bhai and we all would've walked out of RM with you. But..."

Arnav looked down and Payal rubbed Akash's arm, "Calm down"

"Arrey how can I calm down?" Akash shouted.

"Akash, please" NK whispered seeing people looking at them.

.

"Is anything wrong there?" Ayan asked worriedly looking over to the table, "Akash sir looks so angry. What did papa do?"

"Elders talk, we shouldn't care" Ayush said and looked at Aisha.

Aisha took a forkful of pasta and forwarded it to Amara, "try this Ami"

Amara opened her mouth and tasted the pasta. "Hmm....this is so tasty!"

"You need more?" she asked and the girl nodded her head vigorously.

"Bhaiyya taste this" Amara called out to her brother who was looking at the elders worriedly. He looked at her and nodded smiling.

"What's this?" Amara asked pointing to Ayan's plate.

"Garlic bread and tuna bake" Ayan said and took the entire plate placing in front of her, "eat"

Amara smiled cheekily but pouted, "But I don't...I haven't eaten all this before"

Aisha tore the garlic bread and dipped it into the tuna bake. She scooped the tuna and forwarded it to Amara who ate from her hands.

"So yummy" Amara cooed, "Wow, all this food is amazing!"

.

"I know you're angry with us, but I didn't have an option Akash" Arnav said slowly, "How would you feel when someone wants to take Ayush away from you!"

Akash smiled and said, "I'm living 23 years of my life with that fear bhai. Right from the moment Ayush was born di wanted to take him away as her own child. Payal fought back, dadi too. But during his childhood he was highly influenced by di. He loved to spend time with her and even called her ma. He was 5 years old when I explained everything to him, literally everything, like how you guys left and how di wanted to take your baby everything...and that's how Ayush stopped going to her and started spending time with his real mother." Payal looked down and Akash said, "You could've fought her back bhai. You had us, the whole family but you left..."

"Jeeju" Khushi said slowly, "At that point, we didn't know what to do. Even if Arnav ji hadn't decided to leave, I would've left. Because when I came to know that she wanted my baby as her, I didn't want to stay there for even a minute. I just wanted to run away with my baby. So that NO ONE can take him away from me!"

Akash took a deep breath and sighed. Payal asked slowly "Why didn't you guys call us? Didn't visit us? Not even once? Forgot us?"

"What the. How can we forget you all" Arnav said.

"Then why?"

"Because..." Arnav sighed and said, "I love the life we're living now Payal. The low life, the peaceful one. The tension-free life. I love this and I don't want to be back as the great ASR living in his great Raizada Mansion"

"Ayan said you live in Shimla but how did you reach there? What happened after you left the hospital? Tell us everything" Lavanya said.

Arnav looked at Khushi who nodded her head.

Chapter 10

"We both cleared the certificates and left the hospital. We paid the doctor not to disclose any information about our baby" Arnav said, "I took my car and drove away. I just drove...not knowing where we're going. Took many routes that I don't even know"

"In the middle of the journey I felt really tired and it was really difficult to manage the new born baby. So we stopped at a hotel and stayed there for a night" Khushi said, "During night the baby started crying and I didn't know what to do. We tried our best but no..."

"And then the people who stayed in the next room knocked our door. It was a couple in mid 50s. The woman came in and helped Khushi" Arnav said.

"She told me how to take care of the baby, how to massage him, how to bathe him, everything. The whole night she kept telling me what to do and what not to do" Khushi said.

"They asked us what we're doing in a hotel with a newborn infant and I told them everything. Like everything. I didn't know why I did that but I felt I could trust them" Arnav said, "After hearing our story they asked us whether we would like to come and stay with them for a few days"

"They lived in a small village in Shimla. Me and Arnav ji needed to away for a while and we agreed to them. And that's how we reached Shimla" Khushi said.

"They lived in a small house. They gave us shelter and soon we became a family. Their son had passed away when he was 20 years old and are of their own. We call them amma and appa. A few years later Amara was born and she and Ayan call them dadi and dadu" Arnav said, "I expanded their house; built a new section which we converted to a restaurant. Khushi handles it. While I has a tailoring shop. I stitch clothes like I used to do in the beginning days of AR. I love it" he finished smiling.

"Amma and appa passed away few years back leaving behind the house and a small property on Ayan and Amara's name" Khushi said.

"You wanted to be away for a few days and you never returned" Payal said.

"I know my sister" Arnav said shaking his head, "She'll go to any extent to get what she wants. She wanted my baby and I won't let her do that. She made us to choose between you all and our child. And we chose our Ayan"

"Every time we thought of coming back, the face of Anjali comes in mind. How she wanted our baby!" Khushi said in tears, "We cannot think about being away from Ayan. And Amara. So...we stayed back for them!"

"They've grown up now" Akash whispered, "Can't you come back now?"

"Does she live there with you all?" Arnav asked.

They nodded looking down.

"Has she changed?"

"No" NK whispered.

"Then what makes you think that we'll come back?" Arnav asked.

"Bhai..."

"This is my life now Akash. This is my family. Our little world. And we're happy there. I love this life, not the one I used to live as the powerful ASR" Arnav said shaking his head.

"Fine then. At least stay in contact with us" Lavanya said.

Arnav and Khushi nodded and Payal said, "You're going back to Shimla?"

Arshi nodded and NK said, "Can't you stay back? For a few days at least?"

"Amara has her exams" Khushi said, "She is in 12th"

"When does it end?"

"Next week"

"After that it's vacation right?" Akash asked. Arnav nodded and Akash said, "Okay then. After her exams you're gonna come back and stay with us"

"Akash come on..."

"For a few days. Till Amara's holidays ends" Akash begged.

"But in RM..."

"It's your house" Akash cried in irritation, "Why are you being away? Scared of that woman?"

"No" Arnav said, "I'm not scared. I'm fed up. I don't want to face any drama."

"If you love us, you're gonna come and stay at Raizada mansion" Akash said firmly.

"Jeeju please..."

"I don't wanna hear anything" Akash said firmly.

"And what about Ayan and Amara? You're gonna tell them the truth?" Payal asked, "Shouldn't Ayan know that the company where he is doing his internship actually belongs to his father. Shouldn't Amara know that the food she is relishing right now used to be your daily routine?"

Arnav nodded no and said, "We raised them as normal kids. We're a middle class family. I don't want them to be in a rich lifestyle."

"They should know. I mean, one day they would know. Aisha already knows and if she slips? What if she accidently tells Ayan?" Lavanya said, "it's better if you reveal it to him rather than knowing it from another person!"

Arnav and Khushi looked at each other and then at Lavanya. Arnav sighed and said, "Fine"

"When are you leaving?" NK asked.

"Tonight. Train is at 8pm" Khushi said.

.

.

"How do you know Raizadas?" Ayan asked frowning as he sat with his family in the railway station.

"Woh...main..." Arnav stammered and Khushi, "Ayan, woh Akash hai na ...he is your father's brother"

"WHAT?" Ayan and Amara screamed.

"Shhh" Arnav hissed seeing people looking at them hearing the shout.

"And Payal is my sister" Khushi said.

"You're Payal aunty's sister? I mean, oh my god!" Amara cried.

"You are...you're Akash sir's brother?" Ayan cried in disbelief, "I mean...oh yes, Raizada! You're a Raizada!"

"Arnav Singh Raizada" Amara said his full name, "Matlab, papa you're rich?"

Ayan gasped and said, "Matlab Raizada Mansion is yours?"

"Matlab you're living poor while you're actually a millionaire?" Amara asked.

"And AR? If Akash sir is your brother then AR must be....oh god!" Ayan whispered, "AR was made by Akash sir's brother ASR. ASR!"

"ASR...matlab Arnav Singh Raizada?" Amara gasped.

"Papa!" Ayan whispered and covered his mouth with his hand.

"Is this a movie?" Ayan demanded, "One fine day you're being told that you're millionaires!"

"Ayan" Arnav said calmly, "Many things happened in the past that we had to leave the house. For you"

The train came and Amara asked, "What happened? What made you leave your family papa?"

"Let's go" Arnav stood up.

"NO" Ayan said grabbing his father's hand, "You're not leaving with an explanation papa. What's all this?"

"We'll talk later. Bye Ayan" Arnav said and Khushi hugged Ayan.

"But listen..." Ayan cried but they got into the train with Amara.

Chapter 11

Raizada Mansion, New Delhi

9.45 pm

The door bell rang and HP opened the door frowning at the late visitor.

"Arrey beta tum?" he frowned seeing the boy who visited for rakshabandan at the door.

"Akash sir he?" Ayan asked and HP allowed him inside.

"Who is it HP?" Anjali asked walking downstairs, "You? What are you doing here?"

"I want to meet Akash sir"

"Time dekha he? It's almost 10. Go home kid" Anjali said crossing her arm.

"I don't wanna talk to you. I wanna talk to your brother" Ayan said irritated.

"Ayan" Aisha called out from the stairs, "What happened? Why are you here?"

"Ah I see. You came to see her, not Akash" Anjali scoffed.

Aisha ignored her and rushed downstairs. "What happened?" she asked holding his arm.

"Akash sir. Where is he?" he asked.

"He is in his room. I'll call him" Aisha said and Anjali stopped her, "No. If he wants to meet him, ask him to come in the morning. Akash must be asleep"

"What's happening here?" Akash asked irritated and reached the top of the stairs. "Ayan?" he asked surprised.

"I want to talk to you" Ayan said from downstairs.

"Come up" Akash said and looked at Aisha, "Aisha bring him to my study room"

.

"So? What is it?" Akash asked sitting before Ayan. NK joined him and so did Payal.

"Dad won't tell me. Nor would mom. So you guys tell me! What's up with you and my parents? They said that you all are a family?" he said.

"Ha...we used to be one happy family" NK said shaking his head.

"So my dad is your brother?" Ayan asked Akash.

"Cousin brother" Akash corrected.

"What happened? Why did they leave? And why...I mean....tell me everything!"

"Ayan I think you should know this from your parents" Payal said softly.

"Nahi, I want to know. What happened that my parents are living in Shimla. If my father is ASR and the owner of AR fashions then why is he living his life as a tailor when he himself is the god of fashion world? I want to know!" he said irritated.

"Fine" Akash said, "Arnav bhai is my father's sister's son. Matlab my cousin brother. And Anjali is Arnav's elder sister. Both of them used to stay at their father's house in Lucknow, during their childhood. But he was not a good man. He cheated on their mother and she committed suicide. He followed her and bhai and di were brought here by my dadi, that means their nani. So from that day they live with us. Years later, bhai started his business with the help of my parents. He named it AR. AR started as a small cloth manufacturing unit and soon emerged into the best fashion house of India. Money started flowing in and bhai built this house. We bought new dresses, new cars, servants...we became rich. He never told his full name anywhere, always used the initials ASR. As years passed by, AR became the best fashion house in the world and ASR ruled the fashion world!"

"Wow" Ayan whispered.

"And then he met your mother" Payal said, "Some events followed and they got married. Di's husband used to eye on Khushi and therefore Arnav ji kicked him out. This caused a huge issue here because di couldn't see anything beyond her husband. She believed that he is innocent and it took NK bhai, Khushi and Arnav ji hell lot of efforts to prove him wrong. They proved the truth that Shyam killed di's unborn child. So di kicked him out"

"After that di became obsessed with the idea of having a child. But she couldn't adopt because none of the adoption agencies could find a clean background on her. She once tried to abort her baby. Somehow this news reached the adoption centre and this added up to her ex-husband's criminal record. So she couldn't adopt! And that was when Khushi ji became pregnant" NK said, "Di used to take care of her very well, like a queen. We thought that di is over Shyam and the miseries. But as soon as you were born, di asked Nannav, I mean Arnav, to give her his baby. She became very violent and angry. Nannav sent us home and then left Delhi with Khushi ji and you"

"So that was what happened" Akash said and leaned back on the chair.

Ayan sat quiet and then whispered, "So, this is my father's house?" he looked up and around the big room.

"Your house" Akash corrected him.

Ayan looked down and NK said, "We really want them back here Ayan. But they won't come. They don't like to face Anjali di"

"Why do you still have her here?" Ayan asked.

"What can we do?" Akash shrugged.

"Kick her out, if you hate her so much" Ayan said shrugging.

"It's not so easy Ayan" Akash said shaking his head, "It's easy to tell that. But if I kick her out and if she goes to police? She has a limp. She is a woman. And we'll be the bad people who kicked out a woman out of her brother's house. And it's Anjali. She would make it like we wanted to snatch her brother's property and that's why kicked her out so that they can have her shares too"

"Exactly. She has venom in her heart" Payal muttered.

Ayan sighed and said, "I don't know what to do. I mean, it's a shock. AR is my father's company? ASR is my father? God!"

"Ayan, this is your home. You belong here. You don't have to stay in those PGs when you have your house here" Payal said holding his arm.

"But how can I stay here?" he cried, "I don't..."

"Please for us..."

"No I didn't come here for that. I just wanted to know the truth" he said standing up, "It's between you guys and my parents. So let it be. I won't stay here unless they ask me to!"

"Ayan ruk jao...please...for us" NK said softly, "Please"

Ayan looked at Akash and Payal who had the same face, begging him to stay.

"What'll you tell your Anjali di? And her...the makeup woman...who is she?"

"My mother" Akash said, "We'll manage them"

"What'll you tell them? That I'm the same child she wanted to snatch from her brother?" he asked.

"Yes" Akash said nodding.

Ayan sighed and Payal said, "It's fixed. You'll stay here" she squealed and hugged him tight, "My Khushi's son will stay with me!"

Ayan was taken aback on her hug but soon smiled and hugged her back.

.

.

Shimla

8.30 am

"Amiii...what are you doing up there?" Arnav called out.

"5 minutes papa" Amara called out from inside.

"You have an exam today you idiot!" Arnav said, "Have breakfast. You're getting late!"

"Ami, come out!" Khushi called out as she walked into the dining room with two plates.

"What is she doing in there?" Arnav asked.

"Fashion show" Khushi said rolling her eyes and placed a paratha in his plate.

"Here I am" Amara sang and ran into the living room, "how do I look?" she swirled.

"As usual" Arnav said bored.

"You're going for exams? Who cares?" Khushi said rolling her eyes.

"Ma papa...I tried new hairstyle...see...." She whined.

"Have you prepared well?" Arnav asked sharply.

"Ha" she said meekly.

"Har exam main maths mein bahot kam marks milte ho. Iss baar ache se nahi kiya tho Ami, tumhari maa tume mujhse bacha nahi payega" Arnav said warningly. (You always score less for maths. If you don't score well this time, even your mother can't save you from me!)

"Ji papa" Amara said slowly sat for breakfast.

"Kya dara rahi ho bachi ko" Khushi chided and smacked Arnav's arm. (Why are you scaring the girl?)

"She is concerned about her hairstyle when she should be worried and revising topics for today's exam" Arnav said narrowing his eyebrows.

"Arrey bacchi hai....every girl at this age will be concerned about her hairstyle and many things!"

"Whatever. You better do well this time" Arnav said.

"Of course she will. Haina bachooo?" Khushi cooed caressing her hair.

"Maaa....my hair!"

"See" Arnav said shaking his head.

"Aap chup? You had your breakfast na? Then why are you sitting here? Get out!" Khushi said.

"What?"

"Arrey go to work man! Kya kar rahe ho!" Khushi facepalmed and Arnav stood up.

"Ha jaa rahe ho...bye...bye ami....good luck!"

"Thank you papa" Ami said sipping the juice.

"Ma..." she called out and Khushi looked at her, "Wo, is it true that we're gonna stay with Raizadas? After my exams?"

"Ha for some days" Khushi said nodding.

"Wow" she whispered, "Papa is soooo rich?"

Khushi hummed and Amara said, "Then why doesn't he have money now?"

"Why you need something?" Khushi asked.

"Nahi, woh he didn't allow me and bhaiyya for shopping during last navratri right? Why?"

"You know why" Khushi said frowning, "Bhaiyya's PG rent was pending and he asked papa for money"

"Hmm...if papa is so rich then why didn't he have money then?"

"Papa was rich Ami" Khushi said looking at her, "Now, we're like any normal middle class family!"

Amara hummed and Khushi said, "Aren't you getting late?"

"Ha yes" she said and stood up. Washing her hands, she took her school bag and ran out shouting a bye to her mother.

Khushi watched her going and looked away thinking.

Chapter 12

Shimla

10.35 pm

.

"Kaha de aap? I was so worried" Khushi said worriedly and hugged Arnas as he walked into the house.

"I was at Ramu kaka's house" Arnav said rubbing his forehead.

"Ha usual fights?" Amara asked walking out of her room. Arnav nodded and Khushi said, "How much do they fight? Pramila chichi hates her daughter-in-law so much!"

"And papa and you have to go to their home and play the mediator" Amara said shaking her head, "As usual!"

"How was your exam?" Arnav asked.

"Good papa. I wrote everything" she said happily.

"When is the next one? Tomorrow?"

"Nahi, day after tomorrow. After that EXAMS OVER!" Amara squealed, "And we're going to Delhi na?"

Arnav's smiled faded and he looked at Khushi.

"What? Papa, you promised! You said that after exams we'll stay at your big house in Delhi" Amara said pouting.

Arnav nodded and Amara hugged him, "Thank you papa!"

"Jao, go and study" Khushi said and Amara nodded.

.

Switching off the lights, Arnav climbed to the bed. Pulling the blanket over him, he lied down flat looking up at the fan.

"Should I reduce the fan?" he asked, "is this okay?"

"Ha it's fine" she said and snuggled close to him, spreading her arm over his chest. Smiling he wrapped an arm around her and with his other hand, started to play with her fingers that were over his chest.

"How much days are we gonna stay there at Delhi?" Khushi asked slowly.

"I don't know. I just don't wanna go" Arnav whispered.

"Me too. I like it here"

Arnav hummed and said, "I miss Akash, NK and Payal. But...I don't feel like leaving here"

"We'll come back na?" Khushi asked.

"Of course" he said.

"Ayan called me in the morning. He's moving into RM tomorrow morning" Khushi said.

"Akash must have convinced him. He's such a good manipulator!" Arnav groaned.

"It's okay. Ayan he na....he'll manage"

"I just don't want my children to be around her..." Arnav whispered.

"Woh, I felt...I don't know if this is..."

"Khushi, what is it?" he asked softly.

"Ami is growing up. She is 17. Like any other teenager, she is gonna fall for these things...these rich habits, the rich food, the mansion, the facilities..." Khushi trailed off.

Arnav hummed and Khushi said, "It'll be hard to control her. How do we make her understand that it's not the comforts of a mansion but the limitations of a home that makes us happy?"

"When did I understand that?" Arnav asked, "At the age of 30 when I walked out with you and Ayan with nothing in my hand!"

Khushi hummed and Arnav said, "We'll talk to her. She'll understand but she'll take her time. Let her!"

Khushi nodded and Arnav said, "When you were pregnant with Ayan I had all these plans of decorating his room. At that time I didn't know whether it's boy or girl. I had the interior decorators ready to work on our child's room after he or she is born. I wanted to bring the world down at his or her feet. I wanted to give my child every luxury in this world. But I couldn't even buy him an expensive toy car."

Khushi caressed his chest and said, "It's okay"

"No Khushi" Arnav said chuckling, "I don't regret it actually. I realized how stupid I was. My son didn't grow up with expensive toy cars but with actual human beings. He played in the ground with boys of his age. He enjoyed playing football in rain rather than the video games I had planned to buy for him. I didn't buy him anything Khushi but our son had a wonderful childhood, which cannot be bought by money!"

Khushi smiled and said, "This was something I always wanted you to learn. Right from when I met you, I wanted you to know that not everything can be bought by money. There are things that are priceless!"

Arnav hummed and said, "I could've never bought them their beautiful childhood with money. Look at Ayan and Ami. How happy they are! How...normal they are! I'm glad that we're here Khushi. I like this. Me, you, Ami and Ayan – our little world!"

Khushi smiled and kissed him. "You're the best" she whispered on his lips, "The best husband. The best father. And I love you so much!"

Arnav smiled and hugged her tight. "I love you too" he whispered.

.

.

.

.

Raizada Mansion, New Delhi

10.30 pm

.

"Why aren't you ready for office?" Anjali asked frowning seeing Akash sitting in the living room.

"Today is Sunday" Akash said reading the newspaper. Anjali nodded and looked to her left where Payal was instructing HP to make lunch.

"Aur ha aaloo paratha, bindi, malai koftha, tomato rice, naan, aaloo gobi, paneer Manchurian aur haa...gulaab jamun and jalebi..."

"Woah woah woah" Anjali stopped Payal, "Kiski shaadi he?" (Who's getting married?)

"Arrey, we've guest" Payal said, "Didn't anyone tell you? Ah, you don't belong here, so that's why...bye" she walked away.

"What?"Anjali fumed. She stormed to Akash and snatched his newspaper, "We're having guests?"

"Yeah, someone's gonna stay here with us" Akash said snatching back the newspaper.

"Who?"

"Uncle" Aisha called out running to him, "I've readied the room but there's no bulb in the bed side lamp."

"Oh, but the other lights are there right?" Akash asked.

"Yeah but Ayan needs bedside lamp. He is a bookworm and goes to sleep only after reading book" Aisha said smiling.

Akash chuckled and Anjali cried, "Ayan? AYAN IS GONNA STAY HERE?"

"Aisha do one thing" Akash said ignoring Anjali, "Take the bulb from di's bedside lamp"

"WHAT?" Anjali screamed.

"Okay" Aisha said and turned to go when Anjali held her arm, "DON'T YOU DARE!"

"Why?" Akash smirked, "You don't read books at night, do you?"

"No but..."

"Aisha, take it from her room. And if you need more light, take all the bulbs of di's room!" Akash said.

"AKASH"

"Di, you just need one small bulb in your room" Akash said, "These saris and jewellery you wear is enough to reflect that small light and make it into a huge source of energy"

Aisha hid her laughter and HP burst out laughing from the kitchen.

"HP" Anjali screamed and HP ran away laughing.

"My jokes have improved" Akash said to himself and looked at Aisha who burst out laughing.

"Why is Ayan staying with us" Anjali asked calming herself down.

"Because this is his house" Akash said crossing his arms under his chest.

"What?" Anjali asked frowning.

"This is Ayan's house" Aisha said.

"What is this girl saying?" Anjali shouted.

"Remember the child you wanted your brother to give you?" Akash asked with his steel voice.

Anjali gasped and Akash said, "It wasn't a girl. It was a boy. Ayan. Arnav Singh Raizada and Khushi Kumari Gupta Singh Raizada's eldest son, Ayan Sharma"

"So...this is his house" Aisha said.

The calling bell rang and Payal ran to them. "Ayan is here" she said happily and ran to the door.

Akash gave a look to Anjali and walked to the door with Aisha following him.

Chapter 13

Raizada Mansion, New Delhi

10.00 am

"Ha ma, I'm all settled here!" Ayan said slumping on the bed, "Gosh this house is sooo big. I can't believe that this is dad's house!"

Khushi chuckled over the phone and said, "How is everyone there?"

"Great except the makeup kit and saree ki dukaan" Ayan said.

"Ayan," Khushi said seriously "You stay away from them, okay?"

"I'm not a kid anymore ma. They can't take me away from you. Don't worry"

"Akash told you?"

"Hmm everything. I don't understand why you had to move away. She should go, not you guys. Why did you leave when the one to leave is staying here enjoying the luxuries!"

"It's not that easy Ayan. And plus, it's your father's decision"

"Which you can change"

"Let's discuss this later" Khushi said.

"Fine, where is he by the way? Is he home?"

"Nahi, Prateek chacha's grand daughter is getting married. So Arnav ji has gone to get her wedding dress ready!"

"Haww Priya is getting married. I thought she wanted to marry me!" Ayan cried dramatically, "Priya....she broke my heart! Now who will marry me!"

"Who is Priya?"

Ayan jumped under his skin to find Aisha at the door with her arms crossed under her chest, "Who is Priya?" she asked again.

Khushi burst into laughter and said, "Bye Ayaaaaaan"

"Maaa" he cried and looked into the phone and then Aisha. "Aisha...baby...Priya is..."

"I knew it. You have a girlfriend back home. You're cheating on me!" Aisha cried. She took the glass next to her and threw it on him.

Ayan caught it on time and cried, "Aisha, are you mad? Priya is my neighbor who had a crush on me. She declared that she wanted to marry me and Prateek chacha, her grandfather fixed her marriage with someone else. That's it!"

"Pakka?" Aisha asked narrowing her eyes.

"Ha baba...pakka pakka..." Ayan said pleading.

"Hmm...theek he" Aisha said pouting.

.

.

.

1.15 pm

.

"Ayan" Payal said smiling sheepishly, "I didn't know what you like so...."

"Woah" Ayan cried in disbelief seeing the dining table, "Itna saaara khaana?"

"All for you bhai" Ayush said chuckling.

Akash looked at him and smiled. He looked at Payal who had the same look.

Bhai!

Just the way he used to call his brother.

"Bhai sit down!" Ayush cried and pulled him down to the chair to sit next to him.

"Hey Ayan" Lavanya said and sat on the chair opposite to Aisha. Payal sat next to her and Akash sat on the centre chair.

"Where is Aisha?" Lavanya asked. "She is coming" Payal said.

"Ah everyone's here? Ayan, all good?" NK asked walking into the room and Ayan nodded smiling. NK sat next to Lavanya and looked at the food. "Wow, it's a feast!"

Mami penguin walked to the dining hall and gasped, "Food!" she sat on the chair next to NK and started attacking the food without waiting for anyone.

Payal shook her head and said, "Chalo let's start!"

"Without me?" Anjali asked walking into the room. Everyone looked at her and rolled her eyes while Ayan had her eyes fixed on her.

An unknown anger burnt inside him. Before him was the woman who was the sole reason why his parents had to move away from their family. The reason why his father had to move away from his brothers. The woman because of whom his father always looked sad when he saw him and Amara playing. He always thought that it's his thoughts but now he knew; every time his father saw his and Ami's bond he remembered his sister. The reason why his mother moved away from her sister. And seeing the woman before him constantly reminded him of his parents' fear of losing him.

Anjali smiled as she walked towards the empty seat next to Ayan.

No no no no...don't come here! Ayan muttered under his breath.

"Sorry I'm late" Aisha said panting as she ran into the dining room and sat next to Ayan.

I love you Aisha. Ayan whispered in relief.

"Aisha that's my seat" Anjali said irritated.

Aisha looked up at her and then at Ayan. "Aunty" she said, "Ayan is sitting in my seat. So..."

"So? Get up" Anjali ordered.

Aisha slowly stood up and Ayan stood up with her. "There are so many other seats here" he said pointing to the other three empty chairs. "You can sit there"

"Yeah but this is my seat!" Anjali said and sat down in her seat.

"Aisha sit here" Ayush said getting up from his chair and pulled Aisha making her sit there. "Sit down bhai" he said and patted Ayan making him sit between Aisha and Anjali. He walked to the other side and sat next to Anjali.

"Problem solved? Now can we start having lunch?" Ayush asked.

Akash gave an irritated look to Anjali and nodded his head at Payal.

"Ha" Payal said smiling, "Ayan what'll you have first?"

"Ummm I'll have..." Ayan trailed off and looked at the various dishes.

"I know, badaam kheer" Anjali said smiling.

Everyone looked at her and Ayan looked at the table, "There is no kheer here"

Anjali smiled and caressed Ayan's hair, "I know you love kheer and Payal doesn't. So she didn't make it. But I have made the kheer" she called out for HP who walked to her with a bowl of kheer.

"Yeh lo" Anjali said smiling. She dipped the spoon and forwarded it to Ayan.

Ayan looked at Payal who looked to and fro between Anjali and him.

He opened his mouth and accepted the kheer. Anjali smiled and looked at Payal giving her a smirk.

Ayan gulped down the kheer and turned to the other dishes on the table. He took a spoonful of fried rice and gobi manjurian and ate it.

"How is it?" Anjali asked smiling.

Ayan looked at her and said, "It's good"

Anjali gave everyone a winning smirk and said, "Have more son"

Ayan shook his head and said chuckling, "I accepted it since you extended me food. And we shouldn't disrespect food."

Anjali's smile faded and Ayan said, "First of all, no one starts their lunch with kheer. Kheer is a dessert. Secondly, I don't like badaam kheer. I don't like sweets at all. And thirdly, I'm diabetic and you have added sugar in the kheer. Anyway thanks for the kheer."

He turned to Payal and said, "I love Aloo puri"

Payal smiled and served him. "Spicy he" she said chuckling, "Just the way you like"

"How do you know?" Ayan asked surprised tasting the aaloo puri.

"I told her" Aisha said, "Ayan likes spicy food and hates sweets"

"Waise" NK cried, "Tell me something. How did you and Aisha meet?"

"Ha...even I wanna know" Ayush said.

Ayan chuckled and said, "Aisha joined few months ago as lateral entry to final year classes. It was her first day and she had worn a dark blue kurta and light blue jeans"

Aisha groaned and Ayan laughed.

"What?" everyone asked.

Ayan laughed and said, "Actually the women cleaning staff of our college wears dark blue churidhar matched with light blue bottom. Me and my friends were looking for the cleaning lady to clean our classroom and then saw her"

"They thought that I'm the new cleaning staff and gave me a bucket and broom" Aisha said narrowing her eyes at Ayan.

Ayan looked away and everyone burst into laughter.

"Duffer" Aisha muttered.

"Hey it's your fault" Ayan said chuckling, "Who asked you to wear that?"

"How would I know that the cleaning staff has the same uniform?" Aisha cried.

"What a first meet!" Ayush said chuckling.

Akash looked at everyone smiling and teasing Aisha and Ayan.

'How happy everyone are' he thought to himself, 'It's just few hours that Ayan is here and the whole atmosphere changed' he looked at Payal who was laughing at Ayan's joke. He smiled faintly. This was the first time he saw her laugh so merrily in the past twenty three years.

'I hope this happiness always stays' he whispered to himself and looked at Anjali and mami who were eating their food silently.

Just one day!

Tomorrow bhai and Khushi ji are gonna come here.

Akash took a deep breath. 'I hope everything goes fine and they stays here with Ayan and Amara forever'

Chapter 14

Raizada Mansion, New Delhi

10.00 pm

"Where are you taking me" Ayan frowned as he followed NK to a room. NK opened the room and entered. Ayan frowned and entered the room.

"Why did you..." he stopped his question seeing the photo frame hung on the wall. He ran his eyes along the wall and tables to find numerous pictures of the two most important people in his life.

"This is their room?" he asked and NK nodded.

"Who stays here now?"

"No one"

"It looks clean" Ayan said surprised.

"Payal bhabhi cleans it. She never let this room dust. Or I must say, never let memories dust!" NK said pocketing his hands.

Ayan hummed and walked towards the green recliner.

"Nannav used to love this recliner. It would be here that he'll be found during the day, working on his laptop!" NK said smiling. Ayan smiled and sat on it and looked around the room.

"It looks so different..." Ayan said slowly, "I mean...their room at Shimla and here....it's so different. It's hard to believe that dad and mom had once lived such a life. This room is as big as our whole house!"

"House and space doesn't matter Ayan. What matters is love and care. That's what makes a house HOME" NK said smiling.

Ayan smiled and said, "That's right" he walked to the wardrobe and opened it. "It has so many clothes!"

"It's theirs. Though it won't fit them anymore. And it has faded I think" NK said walking towards Arnav's suits.

"It's Armani suit" Ayan whispered and ran his fingers over the material. "It's still good!"

"Nah it's not as silky and shiny" NK said shaking his head.

"Why is the wardrobe full of suits?"

"Because your father wears only suits" NK said with a duh expression.

"Can I be honest?" Ayan asked putting back the suit. NK hummed and Ayan said, "I have never ever seen my father wearing a suit"

"Can I be honest?" NK said, "I have never ever seen your father not wearing a suit, except when it's night and has his night clothes on!"

"From your words, Papa seemed to be like a hero" Ayan said sitting on the bed. NK sat on the recliner and Ayan said, "The great wall of Arnav Singh Raizada. The one protecting the family. He seems authoritative and powerful. But to me....I don't have such an image of my father. I have never seen such a side of him. For me he is not the ASR...he is...is...my father"

NK smiled and Ayan said, "it's so strange. My dad being ASR. I mean..."

"People change Ayan. May be your father has changed. He has become Arnav from ASR" NK said and Ayan nodded.

.

.

9 am

.

"When will they come?" Payal asked Akash who said, "Max 45 minutes. Mohan has gone to pick them up!"

NK smiled and said, "They are coming home!"

"Who is coming home?" Anjali asked walking into the living room.

Akash and Payal looked at each other and then at NK.

"Ha woh...actually..." NK began when Lavanya called out, "Payal, have you seen Aisha?"

"Nahi. Isn't she in her room?" Payal called out.

Lavanya ran to the living room in a tensed face and said, "I've searched the whole house. She is nowhere to be seen!"

"Arrey don't worry. She must have gone out for some work" NK said.

"Nahi NK bhai" Payal said standing up, "She always informs us!"

"Hello hi bye bye" Mami said walking to them, "Not only Aisha, Ayan is also missing!"

Lavanya looked at Akash who called the security.

"Yes sir" the security said standing before Akash.

"Did you see Ayan or Aisha leaving?"

"Ha sir"

Everyone breathed a sigh in relief and the security said, "They left at night and didn't return sir"

"Night?" Lavanya asked.

"Ha...at 2 am or something"

"Both of them together?" Mami asked.

"Ha mam" the man said.

"Theek he...tum jao" Akash said and the man went.

"Hello hi bye bye looks like the youth wants to be wild and went out late at night!" Mami said shaking her head.

"Lavanya you should control your daughter" Anjali said, "Look how she went out with a man at night. She didn't even return home! I wonder where they both are!"

"Stop it di" NK said angrily.

Akash's phone rang and he took it, "Ha inspector Rathode....what? I'll come now...oh okay...fine..."

"What happened?" Payal asked clutching his arm.

Akash looked down and then at Lavanya. "Woh...inspector called. His men has caught Ayan and Aisha"

"What?" Lavanya cried.

"Err...at night...he said he'll come here with them" Akash said slowly.

"Why did the police take them?" NK asked.

"What will they do then?" Anjali asked in disgust, "Late night...alone...young boy and girl...of course they'll arrest"

Lavanya closed her eyes and looked away taking a deep breath.

"La calm down" Payal whispered.

"When will they come?" Lavanya asked Akash.

"They'll be here in no while" Akash said.

.

"Mr. Raizada"

Everyone turned to find inspector walking in with Ayan and Aisha following them looking down.

"Hello Mr. Rathode" Akash shook hands with him.

"Have a reign on your children Mr. Raizada. It's that they said your name and I brought them here. Or else I would have locked them up!"

"What did they do?" NK asked.

Inspector looked at both of them and said, "Wahi usual things! Romance in the streets! Every night the night patrolling police catches couples like this."

Ayan and Aisha looked away and inspector said sighing, "Let it be. Don't repeat this!" he said and walked away.

Aisha looked at Lavanya who stood stone faced.

"Ma..." she called out slowly.

"Aunty...hum...we went to have....pav bhaji!" Ayan said stammering.

"Ha ma...pav bhaji!" Aisha said nodding her head.

"At 2 am!" Lavanya asked angrily.

"Aunty...please don't scold her. She didn't wanna go. I forced her. I wanted to go and...it's not her fault" Ayan said pleading.

.

"Hiii" Ayan whispered as he sneaked into her room.

Aisha sat up on her bed and said surprised, "What are you doing here?"

"Budhuuu" Ayan hit his head, "Boyfriends often sneak into their girl's rooms!"

Aisha chuckled and said, "So what do you need?"

"Pav bhaji" Ayan whispered.

Aisha looked at the clock and said, "At 2 am?"

Ayan nodded her head like a child, "Let's go na!"

"Dekho it's RM. Gates have security" Aisha whispered.

"So? They won't open if we wanna go out?" Ayan asked.

"Sshhh...dheere bolo" Aisha whispered, "Mamma is next door"

"Oooh"

"Ayan, let's go tomorrow"

"Nahi I wanna go now" Ayan said stubborn.

"Fine" Aisha said and Ayan smiled, "Chalo"

.

"Wow how convincing" Anjali said, "Seedhe seedhe bolo...you both went to take a hotel room!"

"Nahi" Aisha cried and Ayan looked at Anjali in pure anger.

"Aur nahi tho kya...these two..." Anjali stopped herself when Ayan took a step forward to her.

"Now listen carefully" he hissed angrily, "I don't have to give you any explanation but I owe these people here one. If we really wanted to take a room, we wouldn't have gone out to a hotel when we live in the same house. Stop being stupid. Don't you dare make stories and degrade Aisha again!"

"Look Akash, how he is speaking to me!" Anjali cried, "This boy is exactly like his mother. I thought he would have values of my chotte but no...he had to go on his mother....talks and behaves exactly like that bitch!"

"BASSSSS!" Ayan shouted and was about to take a step forward when Aisha clutched his arm and pulled him back.

"Ayan stop....don't..." she whispered and caressed his arm calming him down.

"Di, apologize" Akash said taking a deep breath.

"What? Why should I..."

"APLOGIZE TO HIM" Akash shouted angrily.

"I don't need her apology!" Ayan said angrily and shoved Aisha hands from his arm, "I don't even want to see her" he pointed his finger to Anjali and said dangerously, "If I hear one word against my parents...I'll burn you alive!"

Anjali gulped and Ayan looked at Lavanya and said, "I don't know if you believe me or not but you have to believe your daughter. We just wanted to have pav bhaji and the police caught us calling us lustful youths! We were at police station for the whole night and today morning when the inspector came and asked us our address I told this. And the police got us here!"

Lavanya nodded and said, "I believe you. But this shouldn't happen again. It's that Akash's name made the police bring you back. The next time they won't and it would...tarnish both of your reputation. I don't want my daughter to be called names!"

Ayan and Aisha nodded and Lavanya said, "Go freshen up!"

Both of them walked upstairs and Anjali said shaking her head, "I don't know why you guys always turn a blind eye towards their mistakes!"

"Stop it di" Lavanya said rolling her eyes.

"Why would I? Ayan and Aisha got caught by the police and had to stay in police station for a night!" Anjali cried.

"Police station?"

Two voices spoke up and everyone turned towards the main door.

Chapter 15

Raizada Mansion, New Delhi

9 am

.

"Police station?"

Everyone looked to the door and Anjali gasped.

"Chotte!"

"Arnav bitwa!"

Akash smiled and walked towards the door with NK, Payal and Lavanya following them. But before they could reach and hug them, someone else beat them.

"Arnav bhaiyya!" HP cried and hugged him.

Khushi chuckled and others stopped on their tracks gaping.

"Umm...hii HP" Arnav said and patted his back.

"Namaste HP ji!" Khushi said and HP said, "Namaste bhabhi. Yeh kon?" he asked looking at the girl behind them.

"Ha this is our daughter. Amara" Khushi said and Amara smiled.

"Namaste bitiya" "Namaste" Amara said shyly folding her arms.

HP took their bags and walked into the house happily while the other inhabitants looked at him open mouthed.

"Was he always this jolly?" NK wondered.

"Khushi" Payal squealed and hugged Khushi.

Arnav hugged Akash and NK while Lavanya and Payal cocooned Khushi.

Anjali walked towards Arnav who looked at her and looked away.

"Wait stop" Arnav said withdrawing from his brothers, "What were you talking about police station? Ayan was arrested?"

"Ha chotte he was..." Anjali began when Arnav ignored her saying, "Where is he? Ayan? AYAN!"

Ayan and Aisha ran down the stairs.

"Papa" Ayan cried, "You're early?"

Arnav crossed his arms and Khushi asked narrowing her eyes, "You were arrested?"

Ayan looked at Aisha and then at his parents. "It's a misunderstanding papa"

"Were you arrested? Yes or no?" Arnav asked angrily.

"Ha" Ayan said looking down.

"Woah" Amara gasped, "Bhai got arrested. Did they beat you like they show in movies?"

"Shut up Ami" Arnav and Khushi shouted and Amara giggled.

"Papa I can explain. Me and Aisha went out..."

"YOU BOTH GOT ARRESTED?" Arnav cried.

"Bhai relax" Akash said wrapping an arm around him, "The police had a misunderstanding. It's nothing"

"Aise kaise" Anjali said, "They both went out at night and police arrested them for behaving inappropriately in public. They had to stay the whole night in jail"

Arnav and Khushi looked at each other and Anjali said, "Chotte listen to me. You should punish them severely. How can they do this? Forgetting the morals elders teach them and going out at night for..."

"Where are the rooms?" Arnav asked Akash interrupting Anjali.

"Your room" Akash said.

"And her?" he pointed to Amara.

"Ami can stay with me" Aisha said wrapping an arm around the girl who smiled and nodded.

Arnav nodded and held Khushi's hand. He walked towards the stairs ignoring Anjali who walked towards him.

.

.

.

"It still looks the same" Khushi whispered and looked at Arnav who nodded his head. He lied on the bed and looked up at the ceiling.

"Waise I talked to Ayan and Jeeju. They said that the police arrested them for no mistake of theirs. You know how people are. They see a boy and girl together and assume things!" Khushi said.

Arnav hummed and said, "But why did they go out late at night?"

"Pav bhaji" Khushi said giggling.

"Seriously?" Arnav cried and Khushi nodded.

"Aur kya expect karu?" Arnav groaned, "It's your son!"

"Haww" Khushi gasped and said, "Yours too!"

"Yeah but the pav bhaji golgappa bhel puri traits are from you" Arnav said raising his hands, "I've no role in it!"

"Excuse me, who ate five plates of golgappa in a go?" Khushi asked with her hands on hips, "Admit it Arnav ji, you love golgappa. I know that you and Ami go out secretly to have it but both father and daughter can't admit it aloud that I'm right about golgappas being the best food in the world!"

"Hey we don't. I hate golgappa. Ami too!"

"Ha right" Khushi scoffed.

Arnav hid his laughter and looked up at the ceiling. He looked around the room and sighed.

"Feels so weird! Being here after all these years!" Arnav said. Khushi sat next to him and smiled. "This was your sanctuary. And now you feel weird here!"

"This WAS my sanctuary" Arnav said smiling emphasizing the WAS. He sat up and wrapped his arm around her. Khushi smiled and hugged him. "Now it's you" he whispered and kissed her hair.

She smiled and buried her face in his neck.

"I'm hungry" he said.

"Me too" she said chuckling.

"Chale?" he asked raising his eyebrow.

"Par here?" she asked surprised, "It's Raizada Mansion!"

"So? We're not gonna break our routine" he said laughing.

.

.

"Have breakfast" Payal said and Amara sat next to Ayan looked at the huge table. She frowned and looked at Ayan. Ayan looked at her and the siblings shared the known where-is-it look.

"What is it?" Lavanya asked looking at the siblings.

"Woh, it's Tuesday" Amara said and looked at Ayan.

"So?" Akash asked.

"It's palak day" Amara said shyly.

Ayan rolled his eyes and said, "Ami is crazy about palak. So every Tuesday papa and ma cooks her palak dishes!"

"Papa and ma? ASR cooks?" Lavanya asked surprised.

"Ha he makes the best palak paneer!" Ami said smiling.

"Palak paneer palak puri palak palak palak" Ayan said scrunching his face.

"Chup re" Ami said smacking his arm, "Every Thursday they make aaloo for you. So shut up!"

"Ami have this today! Woh papa and ma are tired from journey na? So they won't be able to cook!" Anjali said smiling and placed the aaloo paratha in her plate.

"I hate aaloo. Give it to bhaiyya" she said pouting.

"Nahi nahi, I'll have....toast" Ayan said grabbing the toast from the table. Amara frowned and said, "But you love aaloo"

"Chup re" Ayan said and took a bite of the toast.

"Here you go princess!" Arnav and Khushi said walking from the kitchen.

Amara looked at them and her face lit up in happiness. "PALAK!"

"I thought you won't cook today" Ayan said smiling.

"Aise kaise?" Khushi said smiling as she placed the bowl of palak paneer before her daughter. "Nothing can change the palak day, hai na Ami?" Arnav asked laughing as he placed palak puris on her plate.

"Yayyy!" Amara squealed and hugged Arnav, "Thank you pa!"

"No hug for ma?" Khushi pouted.

"You're a lazy log. I cooked everything" Arnav said smirking.

"Hawww who peeled the onions?" Khushi cried.

"Who chopped palak?" Arnav raised his eyebrow.

"Who was the one to sauté the onion?"

"Who put salt in the dish?"

"Bas bhi karo yaar" Ayan cried groaning, "Bacho ki tarah lad rahe ho!"

"Say this to your mother" Arnav cried.

"Ayan ask your father to shut up"

"Chup re" Ami said giggling.

"Ha listen to your daughter. Chup re" Khushi said it in Amara's tone.

"Chup re ma ki chamchi" Arnav said.

"You're so irritating" Khushi said huffing and walked to the seat next to Amara. "Uddho" she said to Anjali who was sitting next to Amara.

"I'm sitting here" Anjali said rudely.

"I can see that. That's why I asked you to get up" Khushi said in a duh expression.

"Why should I get up? There are so many seats here!" Anjali said angrily.

"There are only two seats around my daughter. One is taken by my son. Let him sit. Bhai he....and the other is taken by you. So get up!" Khushi said crossing her arms.

Amara looked at Khushi and Anjali and then at brother who blinked his eyes assuring that everything is fine.

"Di get up" Akash said sighing.

Anjali huffed and got up from the seat. She looked at Amara who was looking at her with a puzzled face. Suddenly, changing her expression to a sad broken one, Anjali said in a low voice, "I know you hate me Khushi ji but I just wanted to sit next to Ami. I know you want me to stay away from your children. If that's what you want...I'll not come near them again" she wiped the tears rolling down her cheek and walked away limping. Suddenly she acted a fall and cried, "Aaah"

"Auntie!" Amara cried getting up while Ayan held her down.

"Bhaiyya she fell" Ami said slowly.

"Acting he" Ayan said rolling his eyes. Ami looked at her mother who nodded her head.

"Chalo let's eat" Payal said and everyone sat down to have breakfast ignoring Anjali who was on the floor few feet away.

Chapter 16

Raizada Mansion, New Delhi

3.45 pm

Amara whistled her favorite tune as she hopped through the corridors of the mansion. Looking at the chandelier hung from the ceiling, she ran her fingers on the smooth walls, her sandals making tap sounds on the well polished marble floor. "Itna bada vase!" she whispered as her eyes fell on the flower vase kept near the wall. "I have never seen such a big vase! Haww...a person can hide inside it!" she gasped peeking into it.

She looked to the wall where a beautiful painting was hung. Touching the frame she said, "Woah this frame alone will cost my school fees of a year!"

"Ami"

She turned hearing a voice. Ah the limp aunty who fell in the morning!

"Hello aunty" she said smiling.

"Hello beta" Anjali said smiling as she limped towards the girl, "I heard that you had exams. How was it?"

"Good. How are you? You fell in the morning" Amara asked looking down at her leg.

"I'm fine. Aadat he mujhe" (I'm habitual) Anjali said sadly.

"Kiski?" (Of what?)

"Girne ki! And no one helps me in getting up!" (Of falling) Anjali said looking away.

"Achi baat he na" Ami said smiling and Anjali looked at her shocked. "I mean" the girl said, "You fall and then you get up alone, without anyone's help! That's a great thing. I think your family also wants that!" she finished smiling and touched Anjali's hair, "You have such a beautiful hair! Which oil do you apply?"

Anjali chuckled and said, "If you want I can apply it to your oil too!" she took Amara's hair ends in her hand and said, "You're so much split ends. I think you should cut the ends!"

"Ha I should," Amara said nodding, "But ma cuts my hair. She said she'll do it!"

"Acha chalo" Anjali said extending the packet she was holding, "I got this for you"

"Gift? Kyu?" Ami asked frowning.

"Just like that" Anjali said smiling.

"Nahi...I can't..." Amara said taking a step back.

"Come on...I'm your...I mean I'm like your mother!" Anjali said smiling.

Amara hesitated but took the packet. "Thanks" she said smiling. Anjali cupped her cheeks and smiled nodding her head.

.

.

.

"It's so fun!" Payal said happily as she sat on the kitchen counter next to the stove. Akash, Arnav and NK smiled as they continued their cooking.

"Kitchen moments are the best!" Khushi said sitting next to Payal. Payal giggled and said, "Khushi doesn't this scene remind you of ishqbaaz?"

"Arrey ha...the ShivOmRu moments! Kya mast he!" Khushi said excited.

"Ishqbaaz?" Arnav asked.

"ShivOmRu?" Akash asked.

"Ha woh serial he na! Ishqbaaz! Story of three brothers and their lives. Shivay Omkara and Rudra. Their brother moments are the best!" NK said.

"You watch serials?" Akash and Arnav cried.

"Umm ha" NK said smiling sheepishly.

"Hindi serials!" Arnav and Akash cried.

"So? What's wrong with hindi serials?" Khushi asked and Payal nodded.

"Dramatic!" Arnav said.

"Saas bahu drama!" Akash said.

"But it's fun. It's romantic" Payal said smiling.

"And drama...well we have seen much better drama queens, haven't we?" NK asked raising an eyebrow.

"Ha this house is a daily soap drama" Khushi said sighing.

"Wo tho he" Akash said nodding.

"Waise I wanted to tell you guys" Payal said, "Does Amara know about the past"

"No" Khushi said.

"She should. Di will manipulate her" Payal said.

Arnav and Khushi looked at her and Payal said, "Today at the dining table, she acted like she was falling. She acted like she wanted to sit next to Ami but you became the bad guy and made her away. Amara almost fell for it. If Ayan had not held her down she would have run to Anjali."

"She is just 17 and innocent. Di can easily influence her!" NK said.

Arnav hummed and Khushi said, "We'll talk to her"

"Waise where are they?" Arnav asked looking around.

"They all went out" Akash said, "Ayush is taking all of them around Delhi!"

"Hello hi bye bye, what's cooking here?" Mami asked walking into the kitchen.

"Zeher" Khushi said and Payal held her laughter.

"What?"

"Paneer" Akash said.

"Arrey, you know I hate paneer" Mami cried.

"Yeah but this is not for you" Akash said rolling his eyes.

"No food for me?" Mami cried.

"Mami ji, HP has made some food for you. Kha lena" Khushi said.

"I didn't ask you phati sadi" mami said angrily.

"Ma stop" Akash said angrily before Arnav could react, "Her name is Khushi. You better call her that"

Mami stumbled back hearing Akash's angry tone. "Hello...hi..."

"Bye bye mami ji" NK said cheerfully and held her shoulders taking her out of the kitchen.

"I'm fed up" Akash said banging his hands on the kitchen counter frustrated.

Payal held his arm and Akash looked at Arnav. "Har roz nayi drama" he said exasperated, "Sometimes I wish I could kick them out!"

"Nahi" Arnav said nodding no, "Whatever it is, she is your mother"

Akash took a deep breath and said, "You had to leave because of their mistakes."

"No" Arnav nodded no and Khushi said, "We didn't leave because of them. We left because we wanted to. We could've fought them. We could've shouted at di and mami ji but...what's the use? They won't change and we're fed up of their drama! So we left to make a living for ourselves!"

"And they are here enjoying the luxuries you gave us" NK said looking at Arnav.

"It's fine" Arnav said smiling, "I don't care that they are enjoying in the house I built. They are using the things that I earned. How does it matter? It doesn't make a difference for me!"

"Par bhai it's yours. Your mansion, your business, your name....hell every single object in this house is yours! YOURS! And you're letting them live here. If not for your note, I would've kicked them out!"

.

It's been seven hours that Arnav and Khushi were gone with their new born child. Akash and NK were searching the whole Delhi like mad men in search of their bhai and bhabhi.

"Kuch mila?" Nani asked in tears as Akash and NK walked inside.

Both men nodded no and Payal burst into tears.

"Are you happy now?" Akash shouted at Anjali, "They left because of you!"

"What did I do?" Anjali said in tears, "I just asked him...."

"FOD GOD SAKE DI, GET THIS THING IN YOUR HEAD! IT'S THEIR CHILD! NOT YOURS! AND CHILDREN AREN'T TOYS THAT CAN BE EXCHANGED!" Akash screamed.

Anjali burst into tears and walked up the stairs to her room.

"What is this Akash" Mami said angrily and followed Anjali.

"Sir" security said walking to Akash. Akash looked at him and he said, "The nurse who attended Khushi madam at hospital said that there was a note left at their table. It said your name. She gave it to me!" he handed him a piece of paper.

Akash took the paper and Payal, NK and nani rushed to him.

Akash opened it and read it aloud.

"I'm really sorry Akash. But I have to leave...I'm taking Khushi and our baby. I can't stay there anymore. Just let that my "sister" know that she has hurt me very badly. But I don't think she has realized that she has done something wrong. Whatever, she is no one to me now.

I'm sorry that we're leaving you guys but this is necessary. Nani, Payal, NK and...everyone...take care of them. And them...my dear di and mami ji...I don't know what decision you're going to take on them but I have a request. Do not kick them out of the house. Raizada house is theirs as much as it's mine and yours. Also, if you kick them out what's the difference between you and them? So let it be. Forget everything. Let them be there. But don't let their decisions influence your life. I know that your mother holds high priority in your life but for once, for once, take Payal's side. Coz trust me, one day, when you fall, even if your mother isn't there for you, your Payal will be there. Give her the life she deserves, not the one that she is living under her mother-in-law.

I'm leaving everything that I've built and own under your care. It's you who should handle it all. Take care of AR. Take it to the highest position you can! You can do it and you will! Because you're also an ASR – Akash Singh Raizada.

I know that you're surprised that I'm giving you AR's responsibility when you all know that I trust my Friday man Aman Mathur more in business. I'm not giving you this because you're my brother. But because you have that in you. The talent that you never saw. AR was always known by it's owner's name – ASR. It should continue. The only difference is that it should be Akash Singh Raizada instead of Arnav Singh Raizada.

Do it for me brother.

Yours, Arnav"

"Kya senti note likha dha" (What a senti note you wrote!) NK commented chuckling.

Arnav hid his laughter and Akash smacked NK.

"So I was saying...I always wanted both of them out of this house but you held me back!" Akash said, "Why?"

"Raizada house is theirs as much as it's yours?" Payal quoted his words, "Rubbish!"

Arnav sighed and said, "I know you guys hate them. But I don't"

"WHAT?" Akash NK and Payal screamed.

Khushi chuckled and said, "Hate itself is an emotion. And Arnav ji doesn't feel anything for them!"

"Ha" Arnav nodded, "They are...non existing living beings for me. It doesn't matter to me whether they are living here or not...in fact I don't even care whether they are breathing or not! So it doesn't matter! Their presence make no difference!"

"If it makes no difference, why do you still want them here?" NK asked.

"NK it's not that easy" Arnav said sighing, "It's so simple to say kick them out. Get out. But is that simple? She is my blood sister and a divorcee. On top of that she has a limp. If I kick her out of this house, law will support her and she will be back here again. If Akash asks mami ji to leave, again law will support her and mami ji will be back here. No matter what they did, guys, you have to accept the fact that they are our family!"

"Family" Akash scoffed.

"Yeah" Khushi said, "So the best thing we can do is live our lives and ignore them. Let them do whatever they want. Ignore them!"

"As I said before Akash" Arnav said seriously, "Do not let them decide for you! Live your life!"

Chapter 17

Raizada Mansion, New Delhi

2.30 pm

"What are you doing?" Khushi asked as she stepped to the poolside.

"Playing football" Arnav said as he bent down to the plants.

"Kya?"

"Dikhta nahi he?" Arnav asked rolling his eyes.

"Laadgovernor" Khushi muttered and walked towards him.

"Arnav ji" she called out standing behind him.

He hummed.

"Arnav ji"

"Ha"

"Arnav ji" she called out and he turned to her sighing, "Kya Khushi?"

Khushi smiled cheekily and said, "Nothing"

"Tum...pagal ho gayi ho kya!" Arnav cried and turned to the plants. He sat on his knees and took the garden scissors.

"Arnav ji" she called out again and sat next to him on her knees. Arnav rolled his eyes and cut the dried leaves on the plant.

"Arnav ji" she called out to his ear and Arnav groaned, "Khushi stop irritating me!"

"Arnav ji!" she called out giggling and wrapped her arm around his neck. "Khushi Khushi..." Arnav cried as he lost his balance and fell on her. Khushi giggled and wrapped her arms around his neck tightly as his head hit her shoulder.

"Ouch" he cried and tried to get up but she held him down.

"Kya kar rahe ho Khushi?" Arnav sighed and looked up at her. Khushi grinned and kissed his forehead.

Arnav chuckled and buried his face in her neck. "Kaafi romantic mood mein he..." he whispered and kissed her earlobes.

Withdrawing from her hold, Arnav sat up straight and raised his eyebrows. "What's the matter?"

"What matter? Nothing!" Khushi said shrugging.

"Acha? Yeh sudden pyaar?" Arnav asked.

"Sudden? I always have pyaar for you" Khushi said pouting.

Arnav chuckled and looked around the poolside. She also looked around and said smiling, "Memories?"

He hummed and said, "Poolside was our romantic spot!"

"Was?" she asked raising her eyebrow, "If you're ready then we can change the was to is!"

"Woah," Arnav cried, "RM mein kadam kya rakha....mere billi tho junglee billi ban gayi!" (Entry in RM has made my kitten wild!)

"Chup re!" Khushi said smacking his arm and Arnav laughed. He stood up and said, "Now why are you sitting? Get up!"

"Unromantic fellow" Khushi muttered and stood up.

Arnav laughed and said, "Your son is at the age of romancing. Khushi, you're growing old!"

"Tho? Old people can't have romance?" Khushi retorted.

Arnav smirked and Khushi huffed and looked away.

He walked close to her and bend down to her ears "Now that if you insist..." he whispered and she looked at him.

Arnav bend down a little and scooped her in his arms.

Khushi squealed and wrapped an arm around his shoulders.

"You made a mistake" he whispered.

"What?" she asked in a low voice.

"You called the most romantic husband in the world unromantic! Sazaa tho milne chahiye" Arnav whispered and walked towards the room.

.

.

"I was thinking..." Khushi trailed off as she laid her head on his chest. He hummed and ran his fingers through her hairs. "Ami has completed her 12th. She is interested in fashion designing like Ayan. So I was thinking why don't we ask her to write the entrance and join NIFT?"

"If she gets into NIFT" Arnav said.

"Of course she will. It's your daughter! King of fashion world ki beti hogi princess of fashion world!" Khushi said chuckling.

Arnav hummed and nodded.

"First we should tell her about Anjali" Arnav whispered looking up at the ceiling. Khushi hummed and said, "Jiji is right. She should know"

"Arnav ji" Khushi said sitting up on the bed and Arnav looked at her.

"If Ami joins a college in Delhi, then that means she'll have to stay here" she said.

Arnav nodded and Khushi said, "Will that be a good idea?"

"Ami will easily get dazed by glitter" Arnav whispered and Khushi nodded her head. "If she stays here" Arnav whispered, "She'll...she'll get used to these ways and...she is a teenager; growing age. And she's bound to get attracted to this lifestyle!"

Khushi took a deep breath and said, "She might get spoilt. Might. Ayan is grown up. He knows the value of money. He has seen our struggles. But when it came to Ami, she really didn't feel any financial struggles. It was Ayan who knows it close. So..."

Arnav sat up and took a deep breath, "Let's see. I want Ami to study in the best college and if it's in Delhi then she'll stay here because there's no way that Akash and Payal will let her stay in a hostel!"

Khushi nodded and Arnav said, "And regarding her getting spoilt, we'll see. She'll be here then Akash and Payal will be there. Even Ayan and Aisha are around. So it'll be fine!"

Khushi took a deep breath and nodded.

.

.

.

.

4.00 pm

.

"How was the day?" Arnav asked the children as they walked in at tea time. "Great" Ayan said smiling, "Ayush took us all around Delhi!"

Ayush smiled and Arnav looked around, "Where's Ami?"

"She is still sleeping?" Aisha asked frowning as she, Ayush and Ayan sat on the couches.

"Sleeping? Isn't she with you guys?" NK asked frowning.

"No" Ayan said, "She was tired after the train journey and was sleeping when we left. I thought I would take her around tomorrow!"

"I thought she is with you three" Khushi cried and called out, "Ami...Am i..."

"We didn't find her for lunch did we?" Lavanya asked standing up.

Arnav stood up and walked towards the stairs when Amara called out from upstairs, "I'm here. Coming!"

Seconds later Amara hopped down the stairs and twirled, "How do I look?"

"Woah...new dress?" Ayan asked smiling as his sister giggled and twirled in pale pink ankle length gown with dark pink lace tied around her waist.

"Ha Anjali aunty gave me. Nice na?" she said happily.

Everyone's smile vanished and Khushi looked at Arnav.

"Nice" Arnav said slowly.

"Ami...did you..cut your hair?" Ayan asked looking at her.

Khushi looked at her and Ami nodded, "Yeah the ends. I had split ends so Anjali aunty cut it for me. She made it into layers, see...." Ami asked turning around so that everyone can have a good view on her layered hair.

Khushi took a deep breath and said, "I told you I would cut your hair right?"

Ami turned and shrugged, "Ha...how does it matter mamma? Split ends have been cut off, that's it!"

"That's not it! I told you I would do it. What was the need to go to her?" Khushi asked, her anger rising.

"Khushi..." Arnav called out slowly.

Ami looked at Arnav and then at Khushi. "What's the big deal mamma?" she asked slowly and looked at Arnav who blinked his eyes.

"BIG DEAL" Khushi cried.

"What's happening?" Anjali asked walking downstairs, "Kya huva Ami"

"Aunty I told you mamma won't like if I cut my hair" Ami said slowly looking down.

"Arrey you look pretty!" Anjali said wrapping an arm around Amara, "Just like a princess! My rajkumari!"

Arnav and Khushi looked at her shocked.

Payal rose to talk when Arnav said, "Let's have tea"

Khushi looked at him and Arnav held her hand. "Not now" he whispered.

"Listen I'm..." Khushi hissed when Arnav whispered, "I'll talk to her. But not now."

Khushi took a deep breath and walked away.

.

.

Chapter 18

.

Raizada Mansion, New Delhi

7.30 pm

.

Aisha opened the door of her room hearing the knock. "Arrey uncle...aap?"

Arnav smiled and craned his neck, "Ami?"

"Ami...." Aisha called out and moved from the door, "Come in uncle"

Arnav smiled and walked inside. Amara got out from the bed and walked towards him. "Ha papa...what happened?"

"I want to talk to you. An urgent matter" Arnav said seriously.

"I'll leave" Aisha said and left the room closing the door.

"Kya huva papa?" Ami asked slowly.

"Ami listen to me very carefully. You have to stay away from Anjali" Arnav said slowly, "So many things have happened in the past which I'll explain later. But for now, just remember this, she wanted to take away your bhai from me and your mother! This was..."

"The reason why you both left this house to Shimla" Ami completed.

"How do you know?" Arnav asked surprised.

"She told me everything papa" Amara said smiling.

"Who?"

"Anjali aunty"

"What?" Arnav cried.

"Ha she told me how her husband used to eye mamma. Then you kicked him out. She lost her baby and thus she wanted to take away bhaiyya, your and mamma's first child. She told me!" Amara said calmly.

"And still you're with her?" Arnav asked frowning.

"I'm not with her papa. It's not about taking sides. She is repenting. She is truly guilty about what she did. And..."

"Stop right there" Arnav hissed, "What do you mean by she is truly repenting? She fed you this right?"

"I can see that! She has kindness in her eyes" Amara said.

"Ami listen to me" Arnav hissed angrily, "When you look at her you see your reflection in her eyes that's all! She is not repenting! She is not guilty! And right now she is trying to take you away from me and Khushi!"

"But papa it's not..."

"Stay away from her. Consider this as a warning Amara" Arnav said seriously.

"But..."

"No buts. STAY AWAY FROM HER!" Arnav said angrily.

Amara gulped and nodded.

.

.

.

"Yeh lo" Arnav said angrily and threw a packet to Anjali's bed. Anjali stood up seeing it and looked at him.

"Don't even think about impressing my daughter with these gifts of yours! Keep it!" Arnav said angrily.

"Chotte why are you talking like this?" Anjali asked in tears.

"Oh please, yeh drama kisi aur ko jaake dikhayiye...mujhe ne!" Arnav snapped. He walked to her and pointed his finger. Lowering his tone, he said, "The last time I let you go. But not again. If you try to come near Ayan or Ami, I swear on god I'll kill you!"

"Chotte" Anjali said calmly, "Whatever happened 23 years back was really bad. I shouldn't have done that. I was blinded by Shyam and...I did things which I shouldn't have. But now...I truly repent. I love you and Khushi ji. I love your kids. And trust me, I would never want to separate your children from you. Believe me!"

"Ho gaya?" Arnav asked crossing his arms, "Now listen to me. Killing myself is a better option that believing you. And stop calling me chotte. I'm not your chotte anymore! And warning you again, stay away from Ami!"

Anjali looked down in tears and said, "If that's what you want I'll do that chotte. Anything for my little brother!"

Arnav frowned his eyes. Why is she acting so much? He looked at the mirror behind her and took a deep breath.

Amara was standing next to the door.

He turned to the door and found his daughter standing with a sad expression. He looked at Anjali. A sudden hatred rose in him. If Amara wasn't watching, he swore he would've lunged towards the woman and ripped her hair out!

Arnav stormed towards the door and looked at Amara. "What are you doing here?"

"Woh I was walking towards kitchen" Amara said gulping at her father's anger.

"Go" Arnav said and Amara nodded running away.

Arnav turned to Anjali who was watching him with a smirk.

He took a deep breath and said, "I have left my businessman life behind. I just wanna say one thing to you. Don't...I mean...DON'T bring out the ASR in me!" and he stormed out of the door.

.

.

.

.

"That chudail!" Khushi cried in anger, "I'll kill her!"

"Aur Ami is such an idiot! Samajthe nahi!" Ayan said angrily.

"It's not that she is an idiot!" Arnav said slowly and Khushi and Ayan looked at him.

"What's the best way to hide a lie?" Arnav asked, "Surround it with truth!"

Ayan sighed and said, "You're right. Whatever Ami knows about the past is true. That woman told her the past and then told her that she is repenting. Now, unless we prove it to Ami that this woman is not repenting on her doings, Ami won't believe us!"

"Yes" Khushi said nodding.

Arnav sighed and said, "New drama! I'm fed up! Everything was so good until we stepped on to RM!"

Khushi sighed and Ayan said, "You both scold her. Tell her strictly"

"Nahi Ayan" Arnav nodded no, "You know how Ami is. Stubborn. Plus, she won't understand. It's not her problem, it's her age! It'll be difficult if me and Khushi hold up a strict position!"

"You're right" Khushi said, "The more hostile we become, the more she'll go towards Anjali!"

Chapter 19

Raizada Mansion, New Delhi

11.50 pm

Caressing the sleeping girl's hair, Aisha smiled and covered Amy with a blanket. Lowering down the AC since it was too cold outside, she dimmed the lights and took out her mobile.

Suddenly she jerked hearing a knock on the poolside door.

"Who is it?" she asked out loud.

Her mobile pinged with a message and she read it.

Open the door idiot

"Ayan" she muttered and walked towards the poolside door. Moving the curtains she opened the door to his cheeky smile.

"What?" she whispered.

He shrugged and said, "Nothing"

"Why are you here?" She whispered and looked around.

"Let's go out!"

"Look at the time!" she cried.

"So? Chalo naa" he said and pulled her hand.

.

.

.

"Not asleep?"

Arnav turned hearing a voice and smiled at Akash who walked into the terrace. "Nah, you?"

"I had a conference call!" Akash said sitting next to him on the chair.

Arnav smiled warmly and said, "I was so right about you"

Akash frowned and Arnav said, "Handing over AR to you was the best decision I have ever made!"

Akash chuckled and Arnav said, "I've been watching the news for all these years. Every now and then when AR comes up in headlines, my heart swells with pride!"

"Right from the day you left, I worked hard to maintain AR at the same position you left!" Akash said smiling faintly, "Every now and then when AR comes up in headlines, I used to wish if only bhai sees this and comes back!"

Arnav smiled and patted his hand, "I'm so proud of you brother!"

Akash said smiling, "Come back bhai. It's time to return!"

"I can't" Arnav said slowly.

"Why?"

"Because I have left that life behind Akash" Arnav said slowly, "I'm no longer the businessman ASR. I'm Arnav and I love this life. My small world at Shimla! That is my life!"

"But this is also your world. This was your world for many years!"

"This WAS" Arnav said, "It was Akash. It's not now! The peace and happiness I have now is something that I can't explain. During the initial days I found it very strange. A life without AR, without files and meetings, without the work pressure but now...now I don't even miss those. I feel free for the past 23 years! I don't have to satisfy anyone. I don't have to live up to anyone's expectations. I don't have to be the best businessman every year! I can just be myself!"

Akash took a deep breath and nodded.

"I'm so sorry for doing this" Arnav whispered and Akash looked at him. "For my own selfish needs, I've put you through a lot!" Arnav said, "After I left, you looked after AR and our employees. You filled my space. You looked after this family. I'll always be grateful to you Akash! When I chose to run away, you chose to stay! I fled. You fought! I'm so proud of you"

"Don't make it too formal bhai" Akash said patting his brother's hand, "I was quite surprised when you handed over AR to me, when everyone knows that you trust Aman more than anyone in business matters! You trusted me with all this. And all I wanted to do was never let you down!"

"You haven't" Arnav said smiling.

"Just think about it okay?" Akash said, "Whenever you feel like returning, we'll always be here! AR is home bhai. Not matter wherever you wander, when you come back, it's always there waiting for you! AR was and is always your Ayodhya. You're the Ram and I'm Lakshman!"

.

.

.

.

2.15 am

.

"Thank you bhaiyya" Ayan said to the security man who opened the gates for them. The security smiled and Ayan drove the bike into the Raizada premises.

"I wonder what Ramu kaka might be thinking" Aisha said slowly, "We always sneak out during nights!"

"How does it matter?" Ayan chuckled.

"If mamma comes to know, we're dead. She asked us not to go out during nights!" Aisha said.

Ayan parked the bike and she got down.

"Nights are so fun! Uski maza hi kuch alag he" Ayan said.

"Safety too" Aisha said chuckling, "If something happens to me, you're responsible!"

"As if something is gonna happen to you. If someone, accidently, kidnaps you they're gonna bring you back within an hour because you are that irritating and whiny!" he said rolling his eyes.

"What?" she cried and smacked his arm.

"Ab chalo drama queen" he whispered and pulled her arm.

"One sec, the main door isn't locked" she whispered and pointed to the main door which was slightly ajar.

"That's strange" Ayan muttered and both of them walked to the main door.

"Who went out at this hour?" Aisha whispered.

"We'll see in the morning. Go to sleep" he said and she nodded.

.

Aisha walked to her room yawning. Entering the room she locked it and turned to get the shock of her life.

"Amy?" she whispered and looked at the empty.

"Where did she go?" she cried in panic and ran to the bathroom. "Amy?" she called out and opened it to find it empty.

Opening her room door, she ran to Ayan's room and knocked it hard.

"What happened?" Ayan asked as soon as he opened.

"I can't find Amy anywhere" she cried in panic.

"What?" he cried.

"She is missing Ayan" Aisha cried in tears.

"Hey don't panic" he said wiping her tears, "She might be somewhere here. May be in kitchen to get water? Come let's look. Don't cry!"

And after an hour of searching and calling out, the entire Raizada clan realized; Amara is missing!

www.ingramcontent.com/pod-product-compliance
Lightning Source LLC
Chambersburg PA
CBHW070403200726
48294CB00003B/1067